Blood River

A Rick Stone Novel

Phillip Tomasso

This one is for my Family.
I love all of you more than you may ever know...

PROLOGUE

Indonesia Province of Papuas: Wairoku Village along the River Eilanden -- 1982

Oom and Kota walked surefooted through the forest. Their bare feet were calloused like shoe leather. They were naked, but had their penises pushed back into their bodies and their testicals cupped and wrapped with a leaf. Both men were dark skinned, in their late teens, and married with children. They each carried an empty bucket in one hand and a well-crafted walking stick in the other. The walk was second nature to them. They still knew to be mindful while they talked.

Their conversation was no different from what was being talked about back in the village. Rumors and guesses ran rampant. Susilo, older than Oom and Kota, was close to death. The illness that racked his body came out of nowhere and left him in bed in his hut for weeks. Weak and feverish, Susilo was unable to keep food down. The first several days he had spent on his knees vomiting. His wife gave him wet-cloth baths in bed and made sure he was never alone when awake, putting off other responsibilities. until Susilo fell asleep. Caring for her husband was her first priority. No one would fault her for work left until later. It always got done. Just not at the same time everyone else did similar chores. The last several days his wife did not even attempt to feed him. There seemed no point. He remained on his back moaning, and when he talked, it was incoherent.

It was only a matter of time before Susilo died. While the disease he suffered from came on him unexpectedly, the symptoms had been seen many times before. Witchcraft was at the root of the fever. Before dying, Susilo would have a vision. In it, he would get a clear look at the *Khakhua* who cursed him. Then, with his last breaths, he'd have enough air in his lungs to expose the witch among them.

Both Oom and Kota knew better than to voice suspicions while in the village. Out in the forest, it was different. Inseparable since they were infants and best friends while growing up, the two felt safe talking about matters that should never be discussed. They trusted each other. They were closer than most brothers in the tribe.

Setting sunlight spliced through random breaks in the uneven canopy. Rays focused on concise areas of ground vegetation. Kota barely heard the constant squawk of parrots bickering back and forth. It was an evening ritual and you either learned to ignore the penetrating sound, or risked going mad from listening.

Although the Wairoku village was not far from the river, the walk taking mere minutes, Oom and Kota remained always aware. Dangers surrounded them every step of the way, the most obvious being wild boar. Being crepuscular and omnivorous, evening is when they were known to be hunting for food. With sharp tusks, a muscular build and bulky size, they were a threat to most anyone. At up to seven feet long, and between five and seven hundred pounds, a solitary male --if it felt cornered, or threatened-- could kill a person or easily injure a group of people.

Boars were not the only threat in the surrounding and dense rainforest. The Papuan Black and the Taipan snakes thrived in the jungle. Whether they wrapped their 8-foot muscular bodies around low hanging tree branches, or sat coiled in hiding on a rock on the ground, or concealed under Selaginella and Elatostema leafs, they seemed always on the defense and poised to strike. The poison from either would kill a man within hours.

There were additional dangers that intensified once the sun set. Despite the crocodiles that littered the riverbanks, there were also poisonous spiders that wove sticky webs all over the forest. Worse still, Oom and Kota stayed ever on the look out for Yakti tribesmen.

The Yakti were known for brutality that often escalated into unexpected headhunting raids. The walking sticks Oom and Kota carried might keep the men from stepping on a coiled snake, but were limited weapons against the Yakti who were armed with bows and barbed arrows, poison-dipped blow darts, and stone hatchets.

Then, of course, there were all the Wairoku who disappeared during the night and who were never seen again. What exactly happened to them, no one knew for sure.

***

The walk from the village to the river, despite all the apparent and inherent dangers, was a time to get away, a break from everything else. Oom and Kota relished the peace. It allowed them time alone, away from their wives and children. The walk to fill baskets with water for the evening should take half an hour at most. The *brothers* were sometimes gone for over an hour. They would sit by the swift running water and talk of important things, trivial topics, or remain silent and just bathe in the animated sounds of night creature conversations.

As they emerged into the clearing, out from under the treetop canopy, there was only the top half of the sun still visible. It had begun its descent, sinking behind the mountain range. The humidity was thick. Sweat dripped from their brows. Their otherwise taut, dark, and weathered skin was red and clammy. When they reached the riverbank, they set down their buckets and walking sticks. There was time to walk knee-deep into the river. Splashing water onto their arms cooled their bodies immediately.

Oom cupped his hands and scooped up water. He washed sweat off his face and poured some over his head, wetting his short, straight, black hair. Kota did the same, but then dove head first into the river for a quick swim.

In an instant, the water churned and bubbled. Even with the sun nearly set, Oom saw the water had turned red. He thought a crocodile attacked. He saw dorsal fins. More than one.

"Kota! Kota!" Oom looked around. Kota had not resurfaced. His heart sank. Every instinct told him to turn and head back for the banks. Getting out of the water made the most sense. Instead, he pushed forward in an attempt to run toward the bubbles against the current.

However, the bubbles stopped.

The red in the water was swiftly carried down the river. Oom stood still. Waited. Listened.

"Kota?"

A hand shot up from the now murky depths.

Oom latched onto it and pulled. He used all of his strength to get Kota back onto land.

Placing his friend on a bed of plant leaves, Oom thought he might vomit. Kota's body looked hacked. Chunks of flesh were missing from his thighs and gut. One arm and a foot were gone.

Blood and water seemed to ooze out of each wound.

"Oom," Kota said. It came out in a whisper. His eyes were open but looked suddenly clouded over and lifeless.

Oom looked at the river and shivered. Something was in the water, something dangerous. Something that had now eaten out the soul of his friend, his *brother*.

CHAPTER 1

1982. Rochester, NY

Rick Stone entered the kitchen, pulling the collar down over his necktie. "Coffee made?"

Karen turned away from the stove. "Gee. If there were any coffee at all, where might it be?"

Rick tried to smile. He took a mug from the cupboard. "Found it. Right here in the coffee pot," he said.

"That's where I was going to suggest looking first. You're too smart for me, Rick."

"You making eggs?" As soon as he said it, he regretted it.

"Are you kidding me?" Karen held up a frying pan. Scrambled eggs.

Rick sat next to Jared, who was in his highchair. He watched his son grab and fumble over the dry Cheerios in front of him. "We have to fight every morning?"

"*This* is fighting to you, Rick? This is fighting?" She sighed. "You don't fight. You never fight."

He closed his eyes and placed the palm of a hand across his stomach. "I don't need to get aggravated, not with the meeting this morning."

"You going to wear that tie?"

Rick took a sip of coffee. Bitter. He ruffled his son's hair. He ignored the dig. "I'm kind of nervous. The network hasn't asked for a meeting like this before. Not since we were in talks with them for the show."

"You're nervous because if they cancel the show that you'll have to get a real job." Karen used the spatula to scrape burnt eggs onto three plates. She snatched two slices of toast out of the toaster, plopped in two slices of bread and lowered the level. "Want to butter these?"

Rick stood up. "I've got it."

Karen carried the plates to the table, set hers down and then Rick's, and fork fed Jared from the third plate. "Do you think they're going to cancel the show?"

Rick pretended he'd heard concern, if not sympathy, or at least empathy, in his wife's tone. He was fooling himself. It wasn't there, not toward him, anyway. Not in regard to his career. "We've had three pretty good seasons."

He had no idea how the last two fared.

Rick finished buttering the four slices of toast and set two down for his wife and two onto his plate. He looked at his watch. There was plenty of time until the meeting. When Karen was in one of her moods, which was more and more frequently, he just didn't want to be in the house any longer than necessary.

"Of fishing. A TV show about fishing." She wasn't asking. She was merely stating. She did it regularly. It humiliated him, and she knew it.

Jared pushed the fork away from his face. His mouth shut tight.

Rick salted his eggs. "I don't think he wants the eggs."

"He likes eggs, Rick."

"I didn't say *he didn't like eggs*. I said, 'I don't think he wants the eggs.'" Rick looked at his wristwatch again. "I better go."

"Yeah. You better go." She waved a dismissive hand at him.

Rick scraped his eggs off his plate into the garbage and almost cringed. She'd just made them for him, and he was throwing them away. Jared was right. Even with salt they tasted burnt. Too late now. He picked up his briefcase by the kitchen door, and stopped. Karen wasn't even looking at him. She continued trying to feed their son. "I wish we could fix things, Karen. I don't know how it got like this."

"Got like *what*, Rick? Like what?"

She wanted to fight, always looking for an argument. Rick pursed his lips, hoped it resembled a smile. He knew it didn't. "I'll let you know how the meeting turns out."

"You do that."

Rick kissed the top of his son's head.

"Dada," he said.

"See you tonight, buddy." He moved to kiss his wife. She lowered her head, stabbed a fork into eggs. Rick smoothed his tie with the palm of his hand as he stood up straight. He left the house without another word and walked to his car, contemplating.

It was hard to put a finger on when the marriage began hemorrhaging. Karen hated his job, that was a given. When they met, he fished as a hobby, spent long nights slaving away in a factory. When he won fishing derby after derby, sponsors took notice. Eventually, he was offered a job on television. *Catch & Release with Rick Stone.*

That might have been the start of the decline. While she knew his dream had always been to find a way to make a living doing what he loved, he suspected she never thought it could happen, and so resigned to marry him--a simple factory worker.

In two months, it would be winter. He didn't work winters. They filmed twenty-four shows per season. He was paid weekly, the checks spread out over fifty-two weeks despite being for the most part unemployed from December until April.

It was possible the four and a half months he was home every year bothered her. She often said she felt smothered, that he was always around, and she had no time for herself. That hurt. Before marriage, they could not find enough hours in a day to spend together. Things changed. People changed. Life happened.

CHAPTER 2

Brent Halperin wore his hair long, pulled back, and tied off into a ponytail. He dressed in dark, expensive suits with silk ties. You knew they were silk because Halperin told anyone who would listen, and even people who ignored him. Overall, he was a good enough guy, just a little too full of himself. He considered himself something comparable to a Hollywood film producer instead of the producer of a Saturday morning fishing show that came on after cartoons.

"Stone, how are you today?" They shook hands. They were on the eighth floor of an eight story building downtown. There were some TV sets on the first two floors, and offices from the third on up. Cubicles filled the center area and they were outlined by offices. Mr. Harry Krantz, the network president, had a corner office that overlooked the Genesee River.

"Won't lie, I'm feeling a little nervous. Except for pre-filming meetings each season, I can't remember ever being called to a special meeting with just you and Mr. Krantz," Rick said. He worried he might be sweating. Thought he could feel the beads on his forehead, but did not want to appear apprehensive by wiping them away. Instead, he smiled and pointed. "New tie?"

"This is satin-silk. Virtually no texture. Want to feel it?" Halperin said, holding out the point of his tie. Rick ran a hand over the material and nodded. "Nice, right?"

"You have the best ties," he said. It sounded lame. To anyone else, it would have been an absurd comment. Halperin relished in the compliment.

"Thank you," he said. "I mean it. Thanks."

"Sure," Rick said.

"Well, why don't you come in? Harry's already here. We can get started right away. How does that sound? And trust me, Stone, I think you are getting nervous over nothing. Nothing. In fact, we have a. . .you know what, let's go into Harry's office. We don't want to unofficially start the meeting out in the hall without him. Do we?"

Halperin knocked lightly on the door and pushed it open without waiting for Krantz to respond. "After you," he said.

Rick entered the office. Windows made up the two corner walls. The others were decorated with framed photos of Harry Krantz with famous people, many autographed.

Krantz stood up when they entered the office. His hair was white and thick. He couldn't be over fifty. The professional gray slacks, navy blue sports coat, and tie were a staple in his wardrobe. "Rick. Rick. So good to see you." He walked around his desk to shake hands. "Please, have a seat."

Rick sat in one of the two chairs in front of Krantz's desk. Halperin took a corner of the desk, and drummed a pencil eraser on his thigh.

"Would you like some coffee, water, anything?" Krantz said, sitting in his chair once again. He clasped his hands in front of him.

"I'm good, thank you," Stone said.

"Okay. Then we'll get right down to it."

Rick took a deep breath. He had been trying to figure out what the meeting might be about since he learned of it last week. Now that it was time to *get down to it*, he wasn't sure he was ready to find out what was going on.

"It won't be much of a surprise to learn that we have both good and bad news," Krantz said. With his fingers laced, Krantz resembled a man about to pray. "We've received the numbers for *Catch and Release*, and frankly, they don't look good. Ratings are down."

"Drastically." Halperin set the pencil aside. He'd lost his smile. This was it. The meat of the meeting. The show was sinking. They weren't happy.

"We just completed our fifth year. It was almost like no one watched a single episode."

Rick moved around in his seat, sat forward, and leaned back. This was his career, his livelihood. Truth was he could handle the show being cancelled more than having to tell his wife the news.

She would be quick to throw an *I-told-you-so* in his face. He'd never live it down. He'd never be able to live with her. He laid a hand on his belly, worried he might get sick and throw up the few burnt eggs he'd managed to swallow during breakfast. "So, what are you saying?" He sat forward, leaned an elbow onto the arm of the chair. "What are we saying here?"

Krantz held up a hand. "Relax, Rick, no need to worry. We're just giving you the bad news."

"There's still the good news," Halperin said. The grin returned as he stood up and walked behind the desk. Halperin stood next to Krantz, hands stuffed into pockets.

Rick wanted to smile in return, but the twisting knot in his gut prevented it. "Then let's have it. The good news. Because right now, I can't help feeling like I'm on the verge of being fired. I'm not . . . am I, being fired?"

The executives laughed, looked at each other and laughed again. "Fired," Halperin said. "No. Not at all."

Rick leaned forward again and pressed fingertips together. "Then I don't get it. If the show is tanking, and I'm not being fired, what, ah, what's the plan?"

"Glad you asked," Krantz said.

"Imagine this," Halperin said. "We take *Catch and Release* on the road."

"On the road?"

"People are tired of seeing you reel in four types of trout, three different salmon. Don't get me wrong, you've done some great fishing on the Great Lakes. Educated people about safety and lines, and reels, and laws. In Lake Ontario, especially, but let's face it, it's dry. It gets boring. Viewers watch you talk to the camera about your lures and hooks. Sometimes, you catch something big, and sometimes there's nothing. An hour show of you throwing small fish back into the water," Halperin said. "It's the reason we're losing viewers."

"We want to think bigger," Krantz said. "We want to explode against the competition, and really think *outside* the box on this one. How does that sound?"

He nodded. "I mean, yeah. It sounds great. I just . . . I don't have any ideas. I'm assuming you have something outside the box in mind?"

The smiles again. Rick had a sinking feeling. A producer and a network head smiling at him. It was hard not to feel like chum about to be scooped overboard and fed to sharks.

Krantz opened a manila folder that had been on the desk in front of him. He removed a few 8x10 black and white photographs and a couple sets of stapled documents. Krantz flipped through the photos as if he were seeing them for the first time, and then offered the entire contents across the desk.

Hesitantly, keeping an eye on Halperin, Rick took the materials.

"Please, take a second. Look through the file," Krantz said. "We received this in the mail from a fan of your show. At first, it was just going to get a cookie-cutter reply letter from *you* with one of *your* pre-autographed headshots. The secretary handling those things brought the letter to Brent's attention," Krantz said.

"And once I read it, I gave it right to Harry."

What teamwork, Rick thought. He nodded again, thoughtfully, and then looked down at the photos. He bit his lip and winced.

"Not easy to look at, I know," Halperin said. He held up both hands. "Go ahead, though. Keep at it."

The first image depicted in a glossy, black and white 8x10 was of a dead man. There were missing appendages and giant chunks of flesh gouged from the corpse. Rick lowered the file. Bile crept up his esophagus and burned on its way down when he swallowed. "What the hell is this?"

"Keep looking. Read the attached letter, then we'll answer questions," Krantz said. "It's all in there. The explanation."

Rick flipped through the photos. Each one was more graphic than the last. Close-ups of the wounds, the severed limbs. . .He wasn't sure he could take much more. Finally, he just set the photographs aside and read the letter.

The writer was a guy from Pennsylvania who claimed to watch *Catch & Release* religiously, but was, as Rick had just been informed, getting bored of the same old, same old. The entire first page, however, praised Rick and his angling as well as the network for sticking with the show. He mentioned the fact that he couldn't stomach Lance Crowley's show.

Crowley starred in a nearly identical fishing show on a competing network: *Casting with Lance Crowley.*

"At least he doesn't like Lance," Rick said. "That's a win right there."

Halperin shrugged. "Who does?"

"Don't stop reading," Krantz said.

Rick turned the page to find a clipped newspaper article glued to the paper.

Man killed by unknown monster in the River Eilanden

Rick began to read the article, sitting back in his chair. The grisly account told of a tribal man fetching water for his village when he was attacked in the river. Unknown creatures killed the man, biting off an arm and a foot. News of the attack spread through area villages. With more than twenty reported missing people this year, and now an eyewitness to the most recent river attack, a panic has set in. The villagers, who purport to survive by fishing, are afraid to go anywhere near the water, and village chiefs are demanding Papua authorities rid the river of the creatures --fearing they are angry spirits bent on destroying the people.

The second page of the letter expressed the author's idea about how to make *Catch & Release* an elite programming masterpiece--his words.

Rick read the third page of the letter twice before skimming through the photographs and the newspaper articles again. He set the documents back inside the manila folder and closed it on his lap.

"Your wheels are turning," Halperin said. He wound a finger round and round by his temple. It looked more as if he was indicating something or someone was crazy rather than excited.

"They're turning," Rick said, "but in a million directions. I'm not sure I get it."

"What's not to get?" Krantz said. "It's laid out for you."

"And you like this? You want to do this idea?" Rick wasn't sure he knew exactly what the *idea* was. He did not want to appear disconnected from them, but instead as though they were all on the same page. It was silly. If he didn't follow, he should be able to say so. Instead, he worried more about feeling left out.

"I personally think it's brilliant. Pure brilliance!" Halperin clapped his hands together so hard that Rick nearly jumped.

CHAPTER 3

Rick Stone debated calling his wife after the meeting. There hadn't been time. Both Krantz and Halperin, once they had Rick's buy-in, wanted to start with arrangements. There was a lot to get done and little time. The workday flew by. Skipping lunch, he managed to leave the office an hour and a half early.

On his way home, Rick decided to stop at the corner florist. He bought a seasonal bouquet of autumn flowers, sunflower and fragrant lavender, spiked with baby's breath. He thought about purchasing a new vase as well but didn't. When he pulled up to the house, he stopped just across the street. He shut off the engine and sat for a moment in his car. He stared at the house. A light was on in the kitchen and family room. Nothing out of the ordinary.

What bothered him most was the car parked in the driveway behind his wife's vehicle. That was the problem. He didn't recognize it, but jotted down the license plate number, make, and model. He had no idea what he would do with the information. That didn't matter; he wanted it, regardless.

Rick thought about pulling in behind the car and going into his house. He'd confront whatever he found head-on. That was what he wanted to do, what he should do, but not what he did.

Instead, Rick put his car in drive and drove away. He drove aimlessly around town until nearly 5:00 PM before he returned home.

***

The car was not in the driveway when he pulled up to his house this time. Rick regretted the flowers and wondered if he should leave them in the car. He could always throw them out in the morning, or give them to a secretary at work. The news he was about to share with Karen was going to start a fight. The flowers -- pre-bought-- felt like an admission of his guilt. Perhaps they were, and that was the problem.

He almost laughed at the irony of guilt. Rick didn't want to dwell on any of it, on what any of it meant. It was better to block it for now. File it away for later. He didn't have time for the confrontation of it all. In person or mentally.

Getting out of the car, he tucked the bouquet under an arm and reached across the front seat for his briefcase. Generally, there was nothing useful in the briefcase: a notebook, pens and fishing magazines. In truth, he only carried it because everyone else in the office had one. Oftentimes, he wondered what was inside *their* cases. His prop just followed him to and from work. It sat on his desk while at the office, and next to the kitchen door when home. Tonight, however, he had a copy of the file Krantz had shared with him locked away inside.

He shook his head, knowing the meandering thoughts were just a defense mechanism, a way not to think about how the rest of the night was about to go down. For no reason at all, Rick adjusted the knot in his tie. It was nearly November. There was a crispness in the air that normally invigorated but tonight only caused a shiver. However, Rick was not at all convinced the shiver had anything to do with dropping temperatures.

The kitchen door was unlocked. He walked into his house and set his briefcase down against the counter by the door.

"For a minute I didn't think you were going to come in," Karen said.

For over an hour he'd wondered the same thing.

The kitchen table was set. Jared's highchair was butted up to the table between where he and Karen sat. "Any longer and I'd have to throw the roast out. Be too dry for the neighbor's dog to chew on."

Rick didn't bite. He kept his mouth shut and just unbuttoned the top button on his shirt before loosening his tie and pulling it over his head. "How was your day?"

"No better, no worse than any other. Mostly, Jared and I just occupied ourselves while I cooked and cleaned," she said.

"That's it?"

She stared at him, eyes narrowed. "That's it?"

"Jared in his crib?"

"Playpen. He was napping. I left the television on for background noise. Want to bring him in? I'll put out dinner." Karen opened the stove and using oversized oven mitts removed a pan with a large roast, surrounded by diced carrots and potatoes.

Setting his tie and the flowers on his lounge chair, Rick smiled at his son. A bright spot in the evening. "Hey, buddy. Hey, there."

"Dada." Jared threw his arms up.

Rick scooped his son out of the playpen and switched off the television. "How are you? How's my little buddy?"

In the kitchen, Rick secured his son into the highchair before sitting next to him at the table. "Smells delicious," Rick said, and rolled up both sleeves to just below the elbow.

They ate in silence. The only sounds were made by Jared. He cooed and made bubbling noises while he ate. He squashed vegetables in his tiny palms and ate it off his hands. The bib he wore was useless. He'd need a bath after dinner, regardless.

The entire time Rick wondered who had been at his house. He'd given Karen a chance to admit she'd had company. The roast sat like a block in his gut. He kept eating since it would be easier than talking.

His mind was full. A whirlwind of thoughts spun about inside his brain. He wondered how he'd bring up the meeting. Karen hadn't asked. She either had forgotten, or didn't care. If he could, he'd just ignore the topic. Unfortunately, there was no way he could do that. What had been discussed affected not just him and his career but her and Jared as well.

As he laid his fork and knife down, Rick cleared his throat. "I, uh, I had that meeting at work this morning."

"You could have brought it up sooner. It would have given us something to talk about," she said.

He could do no right.

"Well? What was it about?"

"The show. Our ratings have dropped considerably."

Karen looked up at Rick. She might hate the idea that her husband was a fisherman on a television show, and the fact that she was always looked embarrassed when she told people what he did for a living, but she wasn't stupid. Bills were paid, and they were not exactly crying poor. "You got fired? Don't tell me you got fired. It's almost November. You'll never find a job at the end of the year. No one's hiring. What will we do for Christmas?"

"Karen."

"I'm still going to have to buy something for my parents. There's no way my sister is going to show us up on Christmas Eve. Oh, she'd love that. You out of work and her getting Mom and Dad a better present."

"Karen."

"But she married Bob. Pharmacists aren't exactly doctors, but he's got steady work, making pretty big bucks, too."

"Karen!" he said, and forced a smile, surprised he'd raised his voice at all. It had worked. She'd stopped talking. She'd stopped talking and was now staring at him. Waiting. "I did not lose my job."

"Well, why didn't you say so?" She stood up. "Are you going to want coffee? I don't want to brew a pot just for me."

Rick shook his head.

"Not even a cup?"

"Okay, yes, I'll have a cup," he said.

She rolled her eyes and walked to the kitchen counter. "Don't let me twist your arm. I was just asking."

"I could go for a cup of coffee. Thank you," he said. "But I wasn't done talking."

She rinsed out the coffee pot in the sink and then filled it with water. "Go ahead, I'm all ears."

He thought he'd wanted her undivided attention. Her doing something else might make the conversation a little easier; his part anyway.

"A viewer suggested a way to," he didn't want to say save the show, but searched for the words Halperin had used to give the situation that *positive* spin, "increase viewership."

"A viewer is saving the show?" She added three spoonful of coffee into the paper filter and closed the top on the coffee maker.

He cringed and closed his eyes, counting quickly to ten. "The show didn't need saving." That was a lie. He suspected without the viewer's letter, this might be an entirely different talk. "However, you know Harry. He's always looking to make his shows better. And Brent is a yes man through and through."

"And he always stares at me when we're together. It creeps me out. It's like he's, I don't know, undressing me with his eyes. I wish you'd handle that. I don't appreciate being ogled, and as my husband, I'd think you wouldn't like him doing it either." Karen stood with an empty mug in her hand, a finger hooked through the handle.

Nothing had changed. The fact she might be cheating on him made an impact. He just couldn't decide how the situation was impacted. "I'm going to Papua."

Karen cocked her head to one side. "Excuse me?"

"It's the western half of New Guinea. It's a province of Indonesia." Rick was what many might call geographically challenged. Halperin had shown him where the trip was headed. A chunk of land above Australia.

"New Guinea."

"It's actually just Papua. The country is split in half. Papua, New Guinea is on the east side of the country. It's right above Aust--"

"Why are you going to this place?" She'd set her mug down, coffee forgotten.

"We're cranking *Catch and Release* up a few notches, making it more extreme."

"More extreme how? You fish. You catch fish on a hook and then you throw them back into the water. I've seen the show. I'm not sure there is a way to crank up a television show about fishing. So, why? How long are you supposed to be gone?" The way her arms sat folded across her chest, Rick knew an already long day was about to extend into an even longer night. He'd not be able to ignore it, avoid the fight.

"It's kind of an interesting story. . ."

"How long do they expect you to be away?"

"I leave Monday. I'll be back by the beginning of December." He sucked in a breath and held it.

"A month? You'll be gone a month? Tell them we said no, thank you."

Rick put his elbows on the table, breathed out into his hands. "Tell them we said no, thank you? Karen . . . I don't think you understand," he said.

"I don't understand? Really? They don't understand. You can't take a man away from his family for a month. What am I supposed to do? Be a single mother for the month. What about Jared? You want to leave your son for that long? A child changes drastically in a month. He'll end up forgetting who you are."

"Karen."

"Call Halperin now, and tell him you appreciate that they gave you the opportunity to discuss this major topic with your wife, but a joint decision was made to decline the offer. He'll understand. Creepy or not, he has to know that something like this will kill a marriage," she said.

"There is something in one of their rivers. It's killing men. The, the. . .creature, it burrows holes into the victims. They look like Swiss cheese after. I'm going to fish to prove or disprove a creature exists. I'll be like a detective of sorts," Rick said. It was the first time he'd explained the new angle for the show, and it sounded thrilling to hear it out loud--and not just from the lips of his producer.

"A fishing *detective*?" She snorted and rolled her eyes as she tossed her head back to laugh. It started out sounding simply sarcastic, the way a villain in an old black and white show might laugh, loud and exaggerated. Then her shoulders shook. She turned around facing the counter. The laugh grew and grew until she appeared to be reaching hysteria.

"We're taking a small film crew, a guide, and some tribal men up the river to the village, where I'll spend days and nights with them while I fish for the creature. It will be exciting, and new. There will be danger--"

"Danger? How dangerous will this be?" No concern in her tone of voice. Not toward him, anyway.

"The creature has been reported to--"

"*Bore holes in its victims*. I know. And what makes you qualified to catch this creature?"

"I'm a fisherman," he said.

"And how much more are they paying you for this?" Karen said.

Rick felt his shoulders slouch forward as he became even more deflated. "The show was in trouble, you're right. Ratings were bad enough that, I think if it weren't for this opportunity--"

"Opportunity. You're not getting anything extra, are you?"

"I am, but it's not much." He told her how much extra he was making. It covered being away and travel expenses. It was not substantial at all. The thing was that he kept his job. For that, he was thankful.

"Well, good."

"Good?" Rick smiled. He didn't think the slight increase would make an impact.

"When you tell Halperin no, it won't be like you are turning away a ton of money or anything," she said.

Rick was silent.

"Rick?"

He looked up at his wife.

She shuddered. "You didn't?"

"I've already agreed to this, Karen." He stood up and went to the door. He lifted his briefcase and set it on the table. He spun the combination, unlocked, and lifted the case open. Rick removed the manila folder and set it on the table. "This could really take off. Look through the file."

"I don't want to look through any file, Rick. I want you to call Halperin and tell him you made a mistake. You can't go to Peru."

"Papua. It's near Australia."

"Peru, Papua. It doesn't matter. It's still half way across the globe. Call him. Tell him. That's the end of it."

"I'm going, Karen. I'm doing this."

"Oh you're going, are you? This is what you really want to do, then."

"It is."

"Fine. You go off on vacation alone then, but I want you to know this, I can't promise Jared and I will still be here when you get back."

"That doesn't surprise me," he said.

"Oh, really? And what does that mean?"

Rick walked out of the kitchen.

"I want to know what that means, Rick."

He came back into the kitchen with the flowers and tossed them onto the table. "For you."

CHAPTER 4

Brent Halperin stood at the front of the room. Several items were on the conference table covered with a simple sheet. To his right was Harry Krantz.

In the back half of the room, Rick sat with his film crew. Danny Hughes was the cameraman, a bit frumpy and out of shape and a good forty pounds overweight. Flannels and white t-shirts, loose baggy jeans, and running shoes were all Rick had ever seen him wearing. In his early twenties, Curtis Burnette was Rick's sound guy. He recorded dialogue and monologue, lures hitting the water and the whine of the reel when a fish took off. Joanne Wagner was the show's director. Strawberry blonde hair and a killer smile, she always found new and odd angles to capture the catch.

There were many more people involved with the filming of each show. Krantz was not sanctioning everyone for the shoot. Rick was thankful for the team before him.

Halperin removed the sheet.

Danny got to his feet. "No way, man. No way."

Halperin kept nodding his head. "Yes way, *my* man. Yes way! Krantz approved some spending for the journey, folks. We've got us two state of the art Beta cams."

"Beta cams?" Rick said, missing the excitement that his team seemed to share.

"Dude." Curtis raised his hand. "What about me?"

"We have two of these cameras," Halperin said. "And we want you to handle one of them."

"How's he supposed to film and capture sound?" Rick said.

"These cameras are portable, record video and audio onto a cassette. It's magnetic. You can get just over three hours of film on a tape," Danny said.

"Exactly," Halperin said, pointing at Danny. "And not to fret, Curtis. We still plan to pack your mic and a recorder that you can wear and use to capture extra sound, but a second camera could prove very promising. This is new territory we're crossing here, guys. You are like astronauts."

Rick bit his lip. *Astronauts?*

"We also want each of you to keep a log, a journal. Write down anything you want. Talk about the weather, birds, sounds, or the colors. I don't care what. Just record everything. Use all five senses."

"I'm not much of a writer," Danny said.

"Just do it. Start it with 'Dear Diary,' if you want," Krantz said. "It doesn't mean we're going to do anything with it, but figure it is better to have an overload of material than not enough."

"Your plane leaves in the morning," Halperin said. "If you have questions, now is the time to ask them. Once you get on that river in Papua, communication is going to be *kaput*."

"What do we do about food for a month," Danny said, picking up one of the Beta cams and turning it over and around. He held it like it might crumble in his hands.

Rick cocked an eyebrow. "Seriously?"

Danny offered up a half smile. "No offense, Stone, but I'm not eating fish every day, every meal. Or kangaroo, or lizards, or toucans. Sorry. Not doing it."

"He does have a point," Joanne said. She sat behind a legal pad and pen. There were no notes on the page, but she kept busy tapping the pen on the pad. "I mean we can't pack a month's supply of food to haul along with us. Can we?"

"You can't," Krantz said.

Rick had had no idea what to pack. He'd never been gone a month. The idea of being deep in a foreign rainforest where he wouldn't be able to wash his clothing did not carry much appeal. "There was no way I could stuff thirty pairs of jeans and tee shirts into my backpack. Wearing jeans more than a day or two did not concern me as much as what I've come to think of as *the underwear situation*."

Everyone laughed. "I know there is no need to state the obvious, but I'm going to anyway," Krantz said. "The food is where you find it. We've arranged a guide to be with you the entire time. She was originally from a Wairoku village, but is one of the lucky few to leave at a young age. She has a degree from an Australian university. She speaks many different dialects and several languages. I am sure she is quite resourceful as an educated native and will not let any of you starve to death. We hope."

"Speaking of which," Halperin said. He opened a folder and removed a small stack of documents. "We are going to need you to sign these releases."

"Releases?" Curtis said, reaching across the table and sliding a copy over to himself. "This is pretty thick."

"It's a lot of words that basically say should anything happen to you while in Papua that you will not sue the network. God forbid anything does happen; you're still covered as an employee. We just need to make it clear that there is nothing extra to be expected. Filming on the River Eilanden and Becking River will be the same as filming on Lake Ontario. You break an arm there, you get the same Worker's Compensation benefits as if you broke it here."

"And that's what these documents say?" Joanne said, leafing through the pages.

"Yes," Krantz said. "Legal mumbo-jumbo is wordy."

"And I presume you want these signed now?" Rick said.

"Am I going to want my lawyer to look this over, dude?" Curtis said.

Danny set the Beta cam down and picked up his copy of the release. "I wish you'd given these to us sooner. I mean, we leave tomorrow."

Rick clicked the top of his pen, and bent over the last page of his copy. He took a deep breath and signed. "Look, I don't care what this says. It's an amazing opportunity. I am not going to miss it over an uncrossed "T", or undotted "i". I'm going. I cannot wait to fish for this. . .creature. Can you imagine if we catch the thing responsible and it's some kind of new, never before seen species? National Geographic, Pulitzers, Nobels. . .I'm in. All in."

Danny flipped through one, two, three pages, then set the form down on the table, turned to the last page and signed. "I'm in."

Curtis and Joanne locked eyes.

Rick watched them. He knew the thoughts that must be running through their heads. They had run through his. A million What ifs.

What if we catch a weird disease?

What if we get bitten by some jungle creature and go mad?

What if we develop eating disorders from 30 days of trout?

What if we lose limbs in freak accidents?

What if we die?

Curtis sighed, and clicked the top of his pen. "We going to get famous from this, Rick?"

"I can't say for sure, but I think no matter what, we have a once in a lifetime chance to go out on some adventure that very few people will ever make. A real adventure. Not actors on a TV show. Our TV show will be real. You and Danny will be capturing reality. This is about so much more than just a show on catching fish. We'll be like explorers recording every step of our journey for potentially millions of Americans to watch!"

"Damn, you make that sound grand," Joanne said, and signed her document.

Curtis shook his head back and forth. "No way you guys are going to scarf up all the fame and glory, dudes, and leave me here." He signed his document, as well.

"I think you've got your crew, Mr. Krantz," Halperin said, clapping his hands together. "It's going to be like *Wild, Wild World of Animals*, but with . . . extreme fishing. We are going to revolutionize television with a reality program like this. And I don't know if I'd said this before, but I will be joining you all, as well."

Rick and Joanne made eye contact, and both looked quickly away, suppressing smiles.

Krantz depressed a button on the intercom. "Ms. White? Bring in the champagne." He smiled at each of us. "We're celebrating!"

***

Danny followed Rick back to his office. He still carried the plastic flute filled with a third glass of champagne and a thick folder under his arm.

"I went to the library last night. There are not a whole lot of resources on Papua New Guinea. Or just Papua, for that matter. The country split a while back. Papua New Guinea, they call it PNG, is separate from the half of the country we're visiting. Our half is under Indonesian rule. There are some freedom fighters that want to see that half of the country reunited with PNG as one, stand-alone country. Can't blame them. I mean, we did it with Britain. The guys are bad-ass, I guess, but mostly for their cause," he said.

Rick opened the office door. "Want to come in?"

"Yeah. Sure. That would be great."

Rick went to the small table by the one window he was afforded. "Sit. Enlighten me. What exactly are we getting ourselves into?"

"It's a dense rainforest, like almost all of it. Rivers everywhere. Major humidity. The temps aren't too bad, but the humidity is constant, I guess. So we're going to be sweating pretty good," he said. "I mean, I can stand to lose a few pounds, so I'm not sure I'm complaining exactly.

"The thing that got to me was that the place is crawling with these tribes, like Tarzan people. You know what I mean? They're all naked and living in trees and stuff. They use blow darts, bows and arrows. They have like no idea what civilization is like, at all."

"I wonder if we do, sometimes."

Danny laughed. "I'm not talking philosophically speaking. I'm talking cannibalism; sneak through the forest, catch you, put you on a spit, and roast you like a pig. That's where my being kind of heavy becomes more of an issue. You, look at you! Ain't nobody's going to want to eat you when they have something like me to pick from instead."

This time Rick laughed. "I'm not going to let anyone eat you, Danny."

"So, one of my questions is, what are we going to do about protection?" he said. His smile vanished and his expression went solemn and thoughtful.

"We have a guide. Someone very familiar with the area. You heard what they said in the briefing," Rick said. He leaned back in his chair and crossed one leg over the other. The framed photographs of his family that hung on the wall across from him grabbed his attention. Karen had Jared on a knee. They wore jeans and light windbreakers. It was early fall, and they were having a picnic by the water at Hamlin Beach State Park. Hot dogs and hamburgers on the grill. Seeing the picture brought back memories of the entire day. The memories were captured like a video snapshot in his brain. He could play the scenes out forward and backward and see every detail.

"Rick?"

"What?"

"I said, I don't mean anything by it, but our guide is a girl," he said.

"So?"

"Like I said, I don't care, but is she going to have a gun? Can she protect us from these vicious tribes?"

Rick held up a hand. "Whoa, who said the tribes were vicious?"

"They're cannibals. Eating tourists or fishermen, so that's not exactly hospitality."

Rick bit his lower lip. "I'm sure we're not going anywhere dangerous enough to warrant the need of a firearm."

"I don't know. I'm just a bit apprehensive, I guess. I've been to Canada, Rick. Sixty miles west of here. That's it. Niagara Falls. I'm not well traveled like you. Other than going there a handful of times, I've never been out of the country."

Rick had been to Canada and to the Bahamas on his honeymoon. Nowhere exotic, or fancy, or romantic. He and Karen had oftentimes talked about a European getaway; a month spent touring Italy and England. The plan was always there, the execution never happened. The way things looked now, he wasn't worried about going on vacation to Europe as much as he was worried about finding her home when he returned from this job.

"Here. Keep this information I dug up. Read through it." The file of documents and notes was thick. Danny had certainly done his homework. Rick opened the file and began reading through the pages.

CHAPTER 5

Rick wanted his wife and son to take him to the airport. Karen was not having it. He could not help resenting her for this. He instead said goodbye to them at the house. He held and hugged his son for a long time; right up until the cab he'd called for honked the horn in the driveway. The airport was on Brooks Avenue, and only a few miles from where he lived. They had one car. Karen didn't offer to drive him, and he didn't want to leave their only vehicle useless in a parking spot at the terminal for a month.

"I'll try to call you guys when I can. There are no phones or anything once we're in the forest," he said.

"Okay. Be safe. Have fun." Flat. Emotionless.

His thumb absently spun the gold band around on his finger as he walked out of his house. There was the hint of a coppery taste on his tongue when he tried to swallow.

In the back of the cab, Rick stared at his house as they pulled away. Once it was out of sight, he tried to push it out of mind. He wanted to be focused.

The network handled the bags the day before, getting them tagged and to the airport ahead of time. Only thing he kept with him was the journal and a few pens. Part of him was anxious to document the trip. Another half worried about what meanderings might wind up on the pages.

He was to meet his team and Halperin at the gate at the Greater Rochester International Airport. They were in for a long thirty hours of travel between layovers and connecting flights. The flight from Rochester to Chicago was going to be quick and sweet. However, once in Chicago, they'd have over an hour to wait before they flew over nineteen hours to Japan. Aside from Europe, Rick had always wanted to see Japan. They'd be in Tokyo for over two hours, but that was only going to be long enough to get a meal. From Tokyo, they'd fly to a Timika Airport on the Indonesian island of Papua. No one knew how long they'd have to wait before a charter plane then flew them deep into the rainforest to a small airstrip called Oksibil --which was only miles from the Papua New Guinea border.

Knowing the itinerary, Rick decided to stop at the newspaper stand inside the terminal before meeting up with the rest of the team. He'd been hearing a lot about Stephen King's newer novels. It had to do with a rabid St. Bernard. Sounded kind of stupid. It probably would not do well, but he'd enjoyed the previous books written by the guy, so thought, why not?

Browsing, Rick saw that King had a book of four novellas out. Different Seasons. He didn't see the one about the dog, anyway. He also grabbed the October issue of Time with a money-symbol eating Pac-Man on the cover. He put the items on the counter and tossed in a pack of gum, as well.

"This it?" The man behind the counter said, gathering the three items closer to him.

Rick nodded. He had the file from Danny to review as well. He'd gone through most of it overnight when he'd been unable to sleep. There were plenty of articles and information from missionaries that stayed with the Wairoku in the early 70s.

"Crazy about them Tylenol murders, huh?"

Normally, it must be small talk, Rick thought, but the Tylenol murders had the country riveted. Someone had laced extra-strength pills with potassium cyanide. Seven people were dead.

"Police aren't any closer to catching anyone now than they were in September when this all started," he said. "And even though the product's been pulled, what's to say the wacko isn't just doing this to other items on the store shelves?"

"If you ask me, it isn't someone doing it in the stores. It's someone who works for the company at the distribution level," Rick said.

"Why do you say that?"

"Well, that one lady who died didn't buy the pills at a store. She got them from the hospital pharmacy. She'd just had a baby," Rick said. "Kills the theory the poison's being added to the bottles on the store shelves, but I'm sure police know more about this than I do. Thinking about that gives me a headache," Rick said.

The cashier nodded, eyes never blinking. "I know, right?"

Rick paid for his things, sad that his pun was lost, and walked away. He dropped his journal into the bag along with the items he'd purchased. He didn't have a headache but kept a hand on his stomach. Fishing in a boat was one thing. Flying over an ocean quite another. The time was close. Soon he'd be in the air and on his way half-way across the world in search of possible fish responsible for killing at least one man and potentially many others.

***

When Rick saw Brent Halperin, he shook his head. The man was in a suit. They had thirty hours of flying ahead of them. No one would begrudge khakis and a polo. They shook hands.

"What have you got in the bag?" Halperin said.

"Some things to keep me busy on the flight. A book," Rick said, and was about to show Halperin but noticed immediately that the producer was not listening.

Flattening his tie against a crisply ironed and starched shirt, Halperin waved to someone behind Rick.

Rick turned and saw Joanne and Curtis. He waved to them as well.

"You excited about the trip, Rick?"

"Not about flying, so much."

"No? You don't like to fly? I love it," Halperin said, walked past Rick, and ignoring Curtis, shook hands with Joanne. "Turns out we've got seats next to each other for the entire trip. Imagine that."

Imagine that, Rick thought. Joanne had told him that Halperin kind of made her uneasy. He'd asked her on dates a few times, and she would come up with simple excuses as to why she couldn't go out, never having the heart to just tell him she wasn't interested. It made this whole thing partly her fault. Halperin didn't know any better and thought he still might have a chance.

"Curtis," Rick said, and shook his hand. "Joanne."

"This is really radical," Curtis said.

"The airport?" Rick said, a little unnerved at the moment about the flights, and knew he was taking it out on Curtis by teasing him.

"No, dude. I thought about traveling to Papua all night. I barely slept. I mean, I kind of thought about learning *how* to be a cameraman at some point, but with these Beta cams, and now that I'm actually going to just get to do it? Dude, I'm really digging it. It's so, so, it's. . .righteous."

"Yeah, it is, Curtis," Rick said, and patted him on the shoulder lightly. There was no point in teasing. Curtis wasn't going to get the joke, regardless. "You hear from Danny?"

Curtis shook his head. "We talked last night. He was telling me about cannibals on the island. I was like, no way, dude. Quit busting my chops."

"Curtis?"

"Yeah?"

"There are cannibals on the island," he said, realizing it was just too easy not to tease.

"You're pulling my leg."

Rick held up both arms. "No hands."

"Where's Danny?" Halperin joined them, Joanne at his side.

Rick smiled. Joanne cringed.

"I talked to him last night," Curtis said, again. "He's coming. He'll be here."

"I'm here. I'm here!"

They all turned. By the security area near the gate, Danny hustled toward them with what looked like a purse slung across his chest. He wore black cargo shorts and suede brown construction boots without socks. His army-green tee shirt was visible under an unbuttoned white and red Hawaiian shirt.

"Everyone have their boarding pass?"

They did, and Joanne even waved hers back and forth on display. "Right here."

"Then shall we get on the plane?" Halperin said, although it was not a request.

"Rick. Rick," Danny said.

"Glad you made it," Rick said.

"I almost didn't. I was getting cold feet."

"Worried about flying?"

"Scared shitless about getting arrested." Danny and Rick followed behind the others.

"No one is going to arrest you in Indonesia," Rick said.

"It's not Indonesia I'm worried about."

Rick cocked his head to one side.

"It's the handgun and shells I buried in my underwear in my backpack yesterday, but I made it past security alright just now. I'm guessing cops aren't waiting to ambush me," he said.

Rick stopped walking. He grabbed onto Danny's arm, and stopped him. "Are you just being funny?"

"About what?"

"About what? About putting a gun in your carry-on. That's illegal, and dangerous."

"Is being eaten by savages illegal? You going to have police arrest them when we're out in the middle of nowhere and they're slapping barbeque sauce on your buddy Dan's fatty ribs or drooling over this tantalizing rump-roast?" Danny slapped his rear and raised both eyebrows. "Well?"

Rick shook his head. "I don't believe you. I can't believe. . ."

"Don't lie. Part of you has got to be somewhat relieved just knowing I have it. That *we* have it. That we're not going to be leaving our personal safety and well-being in the hands of a college grad who used to also be a cannibal, or might still be one? I tried being a vegetarian once, buddy. Once. I couldn't make it two days without a Big Mac. I know I am."

Rick started walking again.

"You just won't admit it, but I know you. You are. You're relieved."

"Let's step it up," Halperin said from the ticket counter by the boarding area. The lady in her airline uniform smiled at them. Halperin most certainly told her he was a television producer. He finds a way to work how important he is into any conversation, regardless of topic or duration.

CHAPTER 6

Indonesia Province of Papua

They spent over a day in the air and in airports. The large plane landed at the Timika International Airport. On approach, Rick looked out the window. He saw a city to the south of the runway and a river just beyond.

While he'd wanted to spend days in Tokyo, he already felt his gut twist into knots. Something about extreme fishing in a foreign land made him apprehensive. The plane touched down without incident and Rick sighed, realizing that he had been holding his breath.

Halperin indicated the layover would be minimal before the commuter flight would depart on the final leg of the trip. There would be enough time to use the restrooms inside the terminal while the gear was transferred from plane to plane. Joanne smiled at him as she and Halperin were the first to exit. Behind them, Rick descended the steps carefully. He couldn't help but look around. Surrounding the airport was nothing but dense jungle. It was not very hot out, but the humidity was thick and stifling, and by the time he reached the tarmac, his pits had begun to drip with perspiration.

"Papua is a not home to heavy men," Danny said.

Rick heard Curtis laugh.

He could smell the jungle. He could feel it like a giant being around him, pressing in. Although he had never experienced claustrophobia, he wondered if the sudden tightening in his chest might be a symptom.

"Breathe, buddy. Breathe." Danny hooked thumbs in his the belt loops on his shorts and turned a full 360, scoping out the area. "I don't know. This may be all right."

"Fingers crossed," Rick said.

Danny clapped a hand onto the shoulder strap of his backpack. "I'm not worried."

One other large plane sat parked nearer the terminal, a beast among the single and twin-engine propeller planes around it. "We're getting on one of those," Rick said.

"With the mountains and valleys, the air temperature and the humidity. . .I've got a feeling the turbulence is going to get a bit overwhelming."

Rick tried to shrug, as if the idea of a tiny plane bouncing along over a jungle full of unknown creatures and natives, threatening to crash didn't bother him. It did. The knot in his belly twisted tighter and he winced.

"Breathe, brother. Breathe."

***

Indonesia Airlines flew the group in a twin-engine propeller plane from Timika to Oksibil Airport without incident. They did hit small pockets of turbulence. It was not the turbulence that bothered his stomach, though. It was time.

Rick knew his skin had lost any color and that he must look ashen and sickly. Being away from home, his mind ran wild on him. He could not help but picture his wife with another man. She had the house to herself. Jared was never going to reveal the things he saw or heard. She could put him to bed and have all the time in the world to play house, just the two of them. It hurt imagining this guy in his bedroom with his wife. He couldn't force the images of sex between the two of them out of his brain. It ran like a film on an endless loop.

"You good, man?" Danny said.

Rick nodded. "Just too much time in the air, I think. I need to just get where we're going."

"I hear that."

The second thing that took over Rick's attention was not the take-off, nor the landing on the small runway. Nor was it the fact they were deep in the heart of Papua, skimming the Papua New

Guinea border--and that might as well have been Mars, or Jupiter for how foreign it felt, looked and smelled.

No.

What captured and held Rick's attention was the silence Halperin exhibited ever since they boarded the small plane. The weird thing was that he'd not said a single word to Joanne the entire flight, short at it was. Instead, he'd perched his chin on a fist, and his elbow on the small round window pane, and stared thoughtfully at seemingly nothing the entire time.

Inside the Timika terminal he'd witnessed Halperin on the phone. He'd presumably been checking in regularly with Harry Krantz, delivering updates on their progress. It made Rick wonder if Halperin, in turn, had received troubling news.

"We're here, dude," Curtis said. "I mean, we are halfway across the globe. The globe, man. I feel like an astronaut."

"Why, you pee your pants?"

Curtis furrowed his brow.

"Alan Shepard?"

"Dude, what are you talking about?"

Rick shook his head. "A small leap for man."

"A giant leap for mankind, dude," he said.

Rick pursed his lips, offering up a thin smile. "A giant leap for us."

"You think this is going to really hit big? Like, we'll get famous, or a prime time spot for *Catch and Release*?"

"For this one episode?"

"You think it's just for this one show? We're out here a month, fishing in the rainforest, and you think we'll only get one show out of it?"

"I mean, we might be able to squeak out a couple of episodes, but Curtis, we're not making a habit of this."

"A habit out of what?"

"Traversing the globe. This is a one-time deal. We signed a contract for this." Rick pointed at the tarmac.

"You guys coming in out of this humidity or what?" Danny said. He stood by the door to the terminal.

Curtis walked away. I followed, noticing the dark clouds coming at us. They were split and shredded by various mountain peaks, foreboding nonetheless.

As if to punctuate the spied approach, a crack of lightning danced across the belly of the clouds.

I quickened my steps and ducked under Danny's arm into the terminal.

CHAPTER 7

The first thing Rick did, as he had at the other airports, was find the payphones. He called collect, not wanting to carry pockets full of change. He waited patiently for someone to answer and the operator to say, "I have a collect call from Rick Stone. Will you accept the charges?"

He longed to hear Karen on the other end answer, "Yes. Of course, I will."

No one ever answered, and just like in Chicago, Tokyo, and Timika, Rick hung up the telephone deflated.

Brent Halperin must have spent nearly an hour in the bathroom at the terminal. When he emerged he was a new man, dressed in slacks, a French blue shirt, and slightly deeper blue silk (of course) tie. His hair looked greased and combed back. His smile was all teeth. "I am so sorry to have kept everyone waiting," he said.

"Where are the guides?" Joanne said.

Halperin looked at his wristwatch. "Should be here soon, any minute. Do we have all of our gear? Supplies?"

"Waiting on that, too," Danny said. His backpack was on the floor, wedged between his feet.

"You've been making calls to Mr. Krantz? You tell him we're here?" Curtis said.

"I called him before changing." Halperin fixed the knot on his tie tight to his throat and rolled his head side to side as if to alleviate pent up stress.

"Are you not coming with us?" Rick said.

"With you, where?" he said.

"Into the jungle."

He nodded. "Of course I am. Why?"

"You're wearing Italian shoes and a silk tie." I pointed.

"We're going to meet with a representative of Indonesia. I shouldn't be dressed like it was a weekend at the trailer park. Presentation is everything. We had to sweet talk the government quite a bit to gain permission to not only fish their river, but also to film it. Don't forget, we're going deep into that jungle where tribes think they are the only people on earth. They've rarely seen other humans, much less a group of white ones with cameras. The government was worried we'd unbalance the delicacy of the natural wildlife, if you know what I mean." Again, he adjusted the knot. He did not look comfortable. He looked hot. The French blue shirt already looked wet under his arms. "And after we meet with the representative I'll change into shorts like the rest of you."

"Is something else going on?" Rick said, thinking about how tense Halperin had been on the flight from Timika and the way he'd just stared out the plane's window.

"Like what, Rick?" His teeth ground while he spoke.

Rick looked around. Joanne seemed interested in the exchange, as did Danny and Curtis. "Something happened before our last leg. Is everything okay?"

Halperin nodded, as if he was saying yes, but he dropped his eyes and concentrated on looking at the floor. "I spoke with Mr. Krantz. I've been keeping him updated on where we were, and such. He told me something, and I planned to tell all of you before we left the airport."

"Told you, what?" Joanne said.

"Lance Crowley's on his way. Him and his team."

Rick nearly gasped. "Crowley? How'd he find out about this? The guy that wrote us, gave us the information, and said he couldn't stomach casting with Lance Crowley."

"True, which is why I look like something is wrong, because something is wrong. Someone spilled our lead."

Rick shut his eyes to the first image that flashed across his mind.

Karen.

She wouldn't have told Crowley about this expedition. That would be sabotage. She might not love Rick anymore, might not want their marriage to survive, or thrive, but she wouldn't contact the enemy. She wouldn't sink to traitorous behavior, would she?

He had never thought she'd sink to adulterous behavior, either. And with that thought, he'd been wrong. Proven wrong.

She was no longer the woman he once knew, once. . .loved, but to call Lance Crowley --he didn't believe it. Couldn't. Shouldn't. Maybe, though, deep down he did believe it. "He's going to try to catch the monster in the river before we do?"

"Why else would he be here?" Halperin said.

"We're not going to let that happen," he said. "Guys, we're not going to let that happen, are we?"

The team shook their heads collectively.

"Are we?" Rick said. He spoke louder.

"Dude, are you, like, trying to get us to rally?" Curtis said.

"We're here first. We're going to fish the water night and day until we find the thing responsible. We're going to capture everything on film; record everything religiously in our journals, and we are going to beat Crowley and his crew to the punch!"

"Yeah!" Joanne said.

"We're not going to let Crowley beat us to the punch, are we!"

"No!" It was a uniform response, even Halperin joined in. Curtis shook his head, but he also had responded.

"Now, that's what I'm talking about," Rick said.

***

"I am Try Malik, diplomat in Papua from Indonesia," the dark skinned man said. Decked out in a black suit and tie and with the knot in his tie butted against the base of his throat, he seemed more comfortable with the humidity. The man smiled and shook hands with each of the people on Rick's team and then with Halperin. His English was excellent, but there was an Asian flavor to each of his words.

Behind Malik, however, Rick tried not to stare at the petite woman who wore her black hair pulled back into a tight ponytail. Her brimmed hat cast a slight shadow over large, round, dark eyes and illuminated her features, regardless. Her skin appeared supple and smooth.

She was in everything khaki with shorts that showed off naturally tan legs and shapely hips. When she made eye contact with Rick, he looked away.

"This is Tika Rumakabu. She will be your rainforest guide. She is a college graduate, fluent in seven native languages, and once lived among the Wairoku," Malik said.

"It's very nice to meet all of you," Tika said, flashing a smile full of pearly teeth. She kept her hands clasped together in front of her, and slightly bowed with her greeting.

Rick could not pick out the slightest accent.

"Nice to meet you," Rick said. He regretted it. He did not want to look at the others, confident they all stared at him, saw into him --a crystal view at the thoughts he should not be thinking. "I'm Rick Stone."

"I am familiar with you and your show," Tika said, stepping forward. They shook hands.

"You get *Catch and Release* in Indonesia?" Halperin said, and sounded amazed.

Tika laughed. It came off good natured, not like she was laughing at Halperin. "Oh, no. Mr. Krantz sent a box of footage at my request. I wanted to familiarize myself with the people I'd be guiding."

"So you just saw Rick, then," Curtis said. He looked deflated.

Tika shook her head. "No. Actually, the footage was raw. I saw and heard nearly everything that took place on each shooting for a seasons' worth of *Catch and Release* episodes," she said, smiling.

"Really?" Curtis said. He looked happy. Then his smile faltered, perhaps recalling everything that Tika would have been exposed to watching on the unedited film. More quietly he said, "Oh, really."

Rick could only imagine what went through his soundman's mind. The shenanigans that Curtis undertook while filming a show were endless, from dirty jokes and pranks, to cursing and temper tantrums.

Everyone laughed; everyone except Curtis.

"Mr. Halperin," Malik said, when the laughing settled down. "I want to express Indonesia's appreciation for your television network's interest in the filming of the documentary. As we spoke of before, you are not to interfere with the tribes you encounter. In fact, for safety's sake, you are to avoid contact when possible. That is, contact outside of those contacts arranged by Ms. Rumakabu." He smiled, nodding at Tika. "There are many things to fear inside the jungle. Our country, Ms. Rumakabu, and any other persons or animals encountered are held harmless in the unfortunate event of accidents or death. We are agreed on this, are we not?"

"We are," Halperin said, his jaw tight. "Thank you. We understand the rules."

"Not rules," Malik said. "Laws. Interference with tribes and customs, and overstepping boundaries not meant to be crossed could not only get you and your crew injured or killed, you could also find yourselves arrested and imprisoned.

"It is my job, my *obligation*, in speaking with you--with all of you--this afternoon, that I walk away confident that I have made Indonesia's position on the permissions granted to the entire film crew perfectly clear."

Halperin nodded. "Perfectly."

Prison? Rick swallowed, his mouth dry, wishing he'd now taken a moment or two to read through the contracts before signing.

***

Rain poured down from the sky.

Rick, Halperin, Joanne, Curtis, Danny, and Tika stood by the terminal exit. In silence they watched the rain. The unpaved ground quickly became a goo of mud and muck. Danny and Curtis set large duffle bags by their feet. Inside were the Beta cams, audio equipment, including a book mike and recorder, an endless supply of batteries, and blank cassettes. Rick had taken his bowie knife with serrated edge and sheath from his bag and fit it on his belt to wear on his hip. His disassembled fishing poles, reels, and tackle were safely zipped away. Joanne carried a fifth duffle with a First Aid kit, bottled water, and some food. Halperin arranged to have his two suits stored in a locker room while they went on the expedition. Dressed in shorts, a button down casual top, and t-shirt with running shoes, he looked better suited for the work ahead.

Everyone carried a backpack, filled with some extra clothing, journals, and personal supplies.

"We could end up spending our entire day here waiting for the rain to slow or stop. I don't think it will, but even if it does," Tika said, "it is bound to start again. You are here for the better part of a month. The *Galon beboda* has just started--"

"The what?" Rick said.

"The wet season." Tika smiled, as if silently apologizing for the weather in her home country. "We will take two Jeeps to where my cousins are waiting with our pirogues."

"Pirogues?" Curtis said.

"Handcrafted canoes," Danny said. "The natives carve them out of a tree trunk."

"They put Evinrudes on those?" Curtis said.

Danny walked away.

"What, they don't?" Curtis said.

"I'm guessing we row," Rick said.

"The pirogues have motors. Ours, anyway," Tika said. "However, once we leave civilization, you won't find canoes with motors. We are lucky to have this small airport and motor vehicle escorts. That is something new. Normally it would take weeks combing a path through the Jayawijaya Mountains. With the rain it is often not passable and you would have to turn back."

"Then we are lucky," Rick said.

Civilization. Rick almost laughed. Papua might have cities similar to other countries along the coast, but in the middle of the rainforest, the line to cross out of civilization would be stepping just outside the airport property border.

CHAPTER 8

Rick Stone Journal Entry:

This was a first for my crew and me. Personally, I'd never flown across the ocean. We are in Papua, a province of Indonesia, where something swam from the murky depths of the fast flowing River Eilanden, and attacked and killed a tribesman of the Wairoku people. The unknown creature bit off an arm and foot. The thing I hope to do is find and talk with eyewitnesses who saw the attack.

I am not sure what fish could be responsible. The wounds depicted in the pictures make me think of a bull shark. While the bull shark has been known to travel into fresh water, and Bull Sharks are indigenous to the PNG area, I did not want to jump to conclusions so soon and without gathering all of the facts.

On our journey to find answers, we'll utilize the skills of our guide, Tika Rumakabu, *who was born and raised a Wairoku before venturing out of the rainforest and earning a college degree.*

We're all a bit anxious to get started. The trip here has already been long and tiring. The weather forecast is rain, some rain, and more rain. We have just less than a month to meet the objective. It sounds like a lot of time. Catching and properly identifying the creature responsible will not be easy. The one eyewitness has indicated he did not recognize the fish responsible, other than it was large.

Is it possibly a new species or something prehistoric that has managed to keep its identity a secret from tribes along the river for millions of years?

Our pirogues are tied off to a pier and the outboards manned by Tika's cousins. They know this river better than anyone, and they should. The Wairokus have been surviving off the resources of the river for centuries.

Rick re-read what he wrote before clipping his pen between the pages and closing the journal Krantz had gifted him prior to departing from the states. He knew he'd embellished and over-dramatized some of the writing. The network wanted bigger, better. He planned to give them just that.

Initially, he had not been sure how he'd felt about writing everything down. Surprisingly, it felt *good* putting pen to paper.

Tika had been right. The rain never let up. If anything, the downpour became more intense, fiercer, the closer they got to the river.

There was no way to avoid the rain and do their job. Therefore, there was no way to stay dry. Inside the Jeeps, everyone pulled on a rain poncho. They reminded Rick of the slickers people wore while riding *The Maid of the Mist* in Niagara Falls, only slightly more durable. Slightly.

As if someone had counted down from three, doors on both Jeeps opened. The six of them scrambled out with nowhere to scramble. They were under trees in the jungle, but not so deep the canopy provided much shelter. Tika waved off the drivers, insisting they were all set. Rick felt a sudden pang of unease watching the Jeeps pull away.

The only destination in sight was about sixty yards away where two pirogues were roped off on a long plank pier. Tika's native cousins sat in the back of each, ready to man outboard motors.

Rick did not run toward the pier. He and the others ambled forward. It was not as if shelter from the rain awaited them if they reached the boats faster. He'd envisioned much smaller pirogues, knowing that they were carved from tree trunks. The canoes before him looked to have been carved from entire trees. Each was at least twenty feet long. The motors off the back end also looked bigger and more powerful than Rick expected.

He'd been fishing for as far back as he could remember. His dad started him out in a pond, then off the pier along the Genesee River. Eventually, they went out in boats and pontoons. Every time was exciting, whether they caught anything or not. The times fishing with his father made up some of his best memories. Losing his dad to cancer seven years ago took a toll on his life, left an emptiness inside that Rick knew could never be filled.

The wind picked up. Tall weeds bent with each gust. The rain pelted them hard with large warm raindrops.

Once he reached the pier and stood staring into swift moving muddy water, for the first time he felt an apprehension about fishing. It had nothing to do with current as much as the unknown.

Curtis and Danny unzipped bags and removed the beta cams. They fit a thick plastic cover, like a shower cap over the cameras and began filming. They were on the clock.

With the camera seated on Danny's shoulder, he signaled with the point of his finger at Rick.

"Our team is in the Indonesian province of Papua. We're only miles from the Papua New Guinea border," Rick said, facing the lens.

Danny filmed from a different angle and also panned left and right grabbing up images of the environment: the vast rainforest, the river, the guides in the boats.

"The rain has not stopped since our flight landed. The river already looks swollen. We have our work cut out for us. Within the Eilanden is a flesh eating monster with a hunger for human blood. With any luck, I'll reel her in and help provide closure to a tribe that has lost a loved one to the creature's unquenchable appetite. I'm Rick Stone, and you're watching *Catch and Release*."

Danny lowered his camera.

"Well? How'd it sound," Rick said. "Too thick?"

He shook his head. "Nah, man. That was good. Real good. I even have goose bumps."

"Curtis?"

"I liked it, dude. Scary. I know I wouldn't get up to turn the channel."

"Okay," Rick said. "Let's get some more. How about we introduce Tika? Tika, come here for a moment?"

The woman smiled, revealing some of the whitest and straightest teeth Rick had ever seen. "You want me on camera?"

"Are you okay with that?" Rick said.

She stood next to him, hands together in front of her, and nodded. "Do I look alright?"

Beautiful, Rick thought. "Just fine," he said. "We ready, Dan?"

"One second," Danny said, and readjusted the plastic cover on the camera. "Trying to make sure the lens doesn't get wet. And. . .okay. Go."

"Tika Rumakabu was once a tribal member, born and raised with the people of the Wairoku," Rick said. "Returning home, she has agreed to be our liaison and guide while we fish for what just might be an undiscovered species of carnivorous fish."

Danny gave a thumb up and lowered his camera.

"Okay, I know we have plenty of charged battery packs for these, but I'm still worried about running out of juice. I want to capture everything, but don't want to end up shorting ourselves when we need it most," Rick said. "Curtis you get onto one of the boats and film as we travel to the village. Make sure you get shots of me on my boat."

It sounded conceited, Rick knew. It was not. *Catch & Release with Rick Stone* was about Rick. Fishing. The crew knew this.

"Danny, you ride with me," Rick said. Danny was the main cameraman and had been filming Rick since the show's inception.

"Film while we get on the boats?" Danny said.

Rick nodded, waited for the sign, and then spoke to the lens. "These are pirogues. Essentially, they are canoes. The Wairoku hollow out the tree trunks, and then they heat the wood to bend and shape it. I've never seen a pirogue as big as these, or as well crafted."

Tika directed Halperin, Joanne, and Curtis into one boat. "This is Biak. He will be your driver for most of the trip. His wife is nearly nine months pregnant. She should be delivering any day. The tribe has bets going on which day the baby will actually arrive."

Danny never lowered his camera after capturing every word for video documentation. Rick thought viewers might appreciate the human side of the story. It might prove equally, if not more important to this special than perhaps the fishing. Rick suddenly grasped why Krantz and Halperin had been so excited about this episode. He felt the sudden energy behind the concept as well.

Biak nodded, smiling. Rick had no idea if the man understood English or if he just nodded and smiled because Tika gestured toward him with her hands while she talked.

"And Prai will captain this boat," Tika said.

Danny stopped filming long enough to climb onto the second boat. He held a hand out and assisted Tika. Rick waited for Danny to begin filming again, and then got on the boat last.

Rick could not gauge the ages of the drivers. They could be in their late thirties or early twenties. It was difficult to tell. Their skin was dark and weathered, resembling leather.

Rick said hello to Prai, and offered his hand. The man shook it and, like Biak, smiled and nodded. Danny and Halperin each untied a pirogue from the dock and dropped the ropes in the front of the boat.

"We will head to the village first," Tika said. She spoke loudly, talking over the chug-chug-chug of the outboards. She avoided looking directly at the camera, Rick noticed. "Get you all set up, fed, and rested. There will still be plenty of day to fish if you'd like, or we could start first thing in the morning. It is your call."

Rick knew the reported attack occurred at dusk. He wanted to construct the event as close to identical as possible. If the thing in the river struck when the sun was setting, that was when he wanted to fish. Whatever was beneath the water's surface might be a nocturnal predator, and the chances of finding him in the morning or during the day would slim.

The pirogues headed south-west with the current. Rick noticed the paddles, but was thankful for the outboards. He already felt tired. From reviewing the information sent to the network, Rick knew the attack occurred during the evening. He wouldn't make the call now, preferring to wait and see how long it took them to get situated. Decidedly, he would poll the group about whether they wanted to get to work right away or not.

***

Rick assumed everyone else felt in awe the way he did.

"You'll notice that the distance from riverbed to riverbed changes constantly. The current is fast and in places where large rocks protrude, like over there," he pointed, "whitecaps are visible. Get a look at the size of the leaves on the trees that hang low from the branches. They hover just above the water like umbrellas. I am not an expert by any means on wildlife in Papua, but I would venture hungry spiders and vicious snakes occupy tree limbs along these waters."

The rain fell relentlessly. It spilled from his hair, down his forehead, into his eyes and mouth, and rolled off his chin. He had given up on wiping it away. "I do know that freshwater crocodiles live in the area. The females grow to an average eleven feet long and the males up to nine feet. I'm only five-nine. I don't know about you, but even a four-foot croc would intimidate me."

Rick spotted what looked like men along the bank and pointed. "Who are--"

"Don't point. Those are not Wairoku," Tika said. She shook her head. The way she spoke, Rick wondered if there might be an issue. "There are many different. . .communities in the forest. Too many cultures to list."

"Then how do you know those were not Wairoku?"

"I'm from here, don't you remember? I know who is who the way you might pick out a stranger inside the building where you work," she said.

It made sense. "Are they friendly?"

"Yes," she looked away, "if you belong to their tribe. Pointing or making direct eye contact is interpreted as aggressive and hostile."

Rick made a mental note of the information. He'd be sure to make sure his team was also aware. Nothing since they landed made him feel comfortable. It was bound to be a long month, but the way the hairs along the back of his neck stood on end made him that much more apprehensive about coming in the first place.

The first pirogue with Curtis on board pulled up to a bank. Curtis climbed out with his camera. He put a thumb up and filmed as the second pirogue docked and was tied to a fallen tree that lay half in, half out of the River Eilanden.

Rick stood and helped Tika out of the boat. He knew she didn't need it. If anything, she seemed more apt to help him. It was for the cameras, though. Always about the cameras.

Biak and Prai climbed out last, and each man pitched in at picking up the team's gear.

"You'll notice the ground," Tika said. "Tree logs are placed like a. . .sidewalk along the trails where there is heavy foot traffic. The rain is all season long, heavier now in the late fall, and the mud is difficult to walk in. The logs provide some traction. They are not always effective and can actually become quite slippery, but more often than not, they do help."

Rick looked at Danny, who silently indicated he'd captured everything just explained.

Lightning flashed. Thunder boomed.

"Why don't we get to the village," Tika said. "We can dry off and have something to eat."

CHAPTER 9

Indonesian Province of Papua, Wairoku

Rick Stone Journal Entry:
What resembled bamboo and giant fortified leaf huts made up the Wairoku village. The huts, however, sat twenty to thirty feet in the air. Having the homes elevated keeps bugs away, and as a superstitious race, also protects the Wairoku from evil spirits. Construction is not simple. Each home is built on top of a single Banyan tree, with the tops chopped away. Branches and sago palm covering make up the floor, walls, and roof of each hut. The ladder is designed to shake with each step. This warns the Wairoku of a potentially unwelcomed visitor on the way up.

Buried as deeply as they are in the rainforest, it is not hard to understand why it wasn't until 1974 that the Wairoku realized they were not the only people in the world.

"Tika is leading us over to meet the Wairoku Tribal Chief," Rick said to the camera. "Chief Amu must approve of us before we are granted permission to stay among his people. From what has been explained, a hut has already been vacated for us to use. If Chief Amu gives his blessing then we'll move in for the next several weeks. The challenge before us is meeting the chief and making sure he understands that we are here simply to fish for the killer in the river and *not* to interfere with Wairoku customs and traditions."

Tika walked them to the base of a hut. It was so high in the trees that the bottom of the home was barely visible. Looking up into the rain didn't help any. The benefit was that, where they stood, the treetops and hut homes did deflect some of the heavier rainfall.

The women in the village stood alongside the trees and observed the film crew and Rick but from a safe distance. They wore only something to cover their pubic region. Bare breasts and bone necklaces were displayed. The men, however, captured Rick's attention. He did not think any of them had penises. It looked as if they'd undergone extreme circumcisions.

Tika must have caught him staring at the male genitalia. "The men actually push their penis into the body. They use a sago leaf to cup the testicales. A leaf or a hard shell from fruit found in the forest," Tika said.

"I see," he said, but did not. It was too foreign, and he had questions. How was the penis pushed into the body? Why or how did it stay tucked up inside? For now, Rick figured he would leave the subject alone. He did not feel comfortable launching into such a discussion with Tika. She kept dropping her eyes as if possibly uncomfortable with the topic as well.

The ladder that leaned against the base of the closest tree had rungs constructed with some type of twine or vine. One long vine snaked down from the sky beside the ladder and fell a few inches shy of reaching the ground. The vine began to wiggle.

Tika pointed. "*That* is Chief Amu."

Rick looked up, tapped Curtis and Danny on the arms. "Get this."

"Getting it," Danny said, his camera aimed toward the heavens. He moved to get under the tree in a way that prevented the lens from getting hit with too many raindrops.

Amu descended from the base of the hut. He didn't come down using the ladder. Hand under hand, he shimmed his way down the vine. Rick stared, watching every move, unable to look away.

When the chief was on the ground, he turned around and faced his visitors. Despite the displayed strength, Rick still expected to see a man in his sixties or seventies. Chief Amu had to be in his early thirties, maybe forties. His tightly curled hair was black. His skin was pulled taut against the bones in his face. If not for the dark skin and bone pierced through the nostrils, he'd have resembled a skull with hair. The man was sinewy and lean. The Wairoku people did not have doctors or medicine. It was rare to meet an old Wairoku person, Tika later explained. Middle age was considered ancient.

Four tribal men appeared and stood on either side of their chief. The large men had more meat and muscle to them, and were armed with spears.

"I will translate," Tika said.

Rick ensured both Danny and Curtis kept filming; they were. "Do I speak first?"

Tika nodded. "An introduction would be the first step."

Rick pointed to his own chest with both hands. "My name is Rick Stone. I am from America. This is my film crew. We are part of a television show--"

Tika held up a hand. "The chief will not understand anything about television. It would be better just to give names."

Rick knew he'd been speaking loud and slow. As he moved beside each of his crew, he introduced them. "This is Danny Hughes, and Curtis Burnette. This is Brent Halperin and Joanne Wagner."

Tika repeated the introductions to the chief. The man smiled the whole time. Rick guessed the amazement came from seeing so many white people.

The chief spoke. He looked directly at Rick while he talked. Rick waited patiently for him to finish, never breaking eye contact. Chief Amu talked, and at one point, held his hands up to his face and pantomimed taking a photograph. When he finished, Rick looked at Tika.

"He welcomes all of you to the village. He is excited that help has finally arrived. Message was sent to the Indonesian government; other than some missionaries coming to. . .photograph the body, no chief has responded to their pleas for help," she said.

"We thank you for accepting us into your village. We promise not to interfere with you in any way. We will just be observers as we fish the river for the monster responsible for the death," Rick said. He knew he'd been talking slow and loud, as if doing so would make his foreign words easier for the chief to understand.

After she translated and listened to the chief's response Tika said, "The village has suffered heartache. The loss of so many people is upsetting. Everyone in the village is fearful of the night now. Even our best hunters, though they will not admit it, are frightened by the spirits plaguing the community."

Rick pursed his lips. "I'm sorry. I'm not following. We were told of the single death, of a man who was killed in the river by some type of dangerous fish. I am not sure what he's talking about."

Tika shook her head. "Let me see if I can get a better explanation."

Rick waited. He turned to look at the others in the group. He read the concern on their expressions. Something wasn't jiving, and they all seemed to sense it.

Tika touched Rick on the arm. "I explained to Chief Amu that you are here to fish for the river monster that took Kota's life--"

"Kota?"

"Yes. One of my cousins. He was the man who died in the river."

"I'm sorry."

"I did not know him. Most everyone here is my cousin or a relative in some way," Tika said. "Chief Amu said the death of Kota is very sad. They have no idea what it is in the river. They believe it is an evil spirit or that it was put there with magic by their enemies--forcing them to stay away from the water and trapped on land."

"That makes sense," Rick said.

"That is not all. There is more," Tika said.

Chief Amu talked more. His hands became animated. He motioned to the people all around him. He looked up to the huts and out toward the forest.

Tika said, "Men, women, and children have gone missing over the last several months. Tracking parties have gone out looking for the missing people but have not been able to find any of them."

"In the river?" Rick said.

Tika translated.

Chief Amu spoke.

Tika turned to Rick. "Not from the river, from the forest."

CHAPTER 10

"What is that about? The chief's going on and on about missing people?" Halperin stood next to Rick. Men led them into a hut only six feet off the ground.

"I thought we were going to have to climb a hundred feet to get to a bed." Danny shouldered his way between them.

Halperin narrowed his eyes and watched until Danny was inside the hut. "Rick, what is going on?"

"You know as much as I do," Rick said. "You set this up, not me. Tika is going to get us more information."

"How many people have gone missing?" Halperin crossed his arms over his chest.

Rick refrained from eye-rolling. "I just told you. Tika is getting more information. Look, you just heard all of this at the same time as I did. I don't know what they're talking about. If anything, I should be asking you. I should be demanding to know what you got us into."

Halperin spun around one-eighty. "We should abort. Load our stuff back onto the boats and just get out of here."

"We just got here. Let's not panic. I've done a lot of research. These people are very superstitious. We can't put too much stock into what's been said until we have more facts. Besides, what about the show?" Rick said.

"What about it? I'm not liking this. I knew we were going to the jungle, and I knew we'd be a million miles from civilization, but this is absurd, Rick," Halperin said.

"It was your idea."

"It was Krantz's, not mine. He came to me with the idea. What am I going to say, no? I don't think so. The network makes a suggestion, you go with it. If you don't, there are a ton of producers itching to get a break in the business." Halperin huffed.

His shoulders went up and down as he exhaled. "There's some monster in the water and a haunted forest all around us."

"You don't believe in ghosts, do you?" Rick almost laughed. He kept his composure.

"In the states? No. Out here, it's kind of hard not to get spooked. Look around us. You can't see a foot in front of you once you're in the forest. Forget about the snakes and crocodiles by the riverbanks. What else is out there? What evil things have transpired here over the centuries? Angry evil spirits? It's possible."

Rick remembered the natives he'd seen on the pirogue ride to the Wairoku village. Tika indicated they might be hostile. Halperin had been on the other canoe. He didn't know about them, and Rick wanted to keep it that way. "I can promise you it's not ghosts. Cannibals, maybe, but not ghosts," Rick said. He laughed, knowing it wasn't exactly a joke.

"You're not funny."

Rick shrugged. They were in a foreign country, on strange soil, and were to live among people that had no idea what a television or camera was. There was humor all around if you looked close enough. "We're not going into the forest, right, Brent? We're going fishing. I've done it millions of times. If you want, we spend a couple of days instead of weeks here. We get some great footage trying to hook a monster on the end of my line. Either we land the fish or we don't. We get some film on their customs and practices as they allow, and then we get out of here. I wasn't too excited to be gone a month from my family anyway."

"How did Karen take it? Was she upset?"

"You could say that."

"Okay." Halperin nodded. "Few days. Not a few weeks. It makes more sense. I'm not sure what Krantz was thinking. Why the hell would we need to be here for a month? We either catch the fish or we don't."

"Guys, you have to see this hut. It's not bad. Not bad at all." Danny stood on the small front porch. He kept his hands on his hips. "Aside from the rain, I kind of liking it here."

Halperin climbed the small ladder. "Don't get used to it."

When he was inside the hut, Danny looked at Rick. "What's with him?"

"I have no idea. Heebie jeebies or something."

"You coming in to check out the hut?"

"Where's Curtis?" Rick said.

"He followed Tika," Danny said, and motioned with both arms toward the hut's entrance.

"Maybe later. I want to see what's what," Rick said.

"Suit yourself. The best beds might be claimed by the time you get back."

"See if they have a firm mattress for me, alright?"

He laughed. "Done, boss. Want me to see if they have a dehumidifier, too?"

***

Rick watched Brent Halperin pace back and forth inside the hut. Their gear was stashed by makeshift beds. There were not enough for all of them. There would have to be some doubling up.

There was a knock on the door. Joanne called for them to come in, and Tika stepped across the threshold.

"Is everything okay with your home away from home?" Tika offered a thin smile, as if worried everyone might complain about the accommodations.

"It is very welcoming, thank you for so much hospitality," Joanne said.

Tika looked around at everyone. "If you need anything else, please don't hesitate to ask. Even if I cannot get you everything you want, I will do my best to make sure you have everything you need."

"Thank you," Rick said. "That's very generous. I'm sure we are going to be all set for the time we're here."

"What did you find out about the missing people?" Halperin said. He looked like he might be coming unraveled. Pressed shirt and silk ties were not going to preserve his mental appearance. The man was a wreck.

"May I sit?" Tika motioned toward one of the three-legged stools.

"Please," Rick said.

"Can we film this?" Danny asked.

Tika shrugged and looked at Rick. "I don't see why not. The truth is, the more exposure received the better it might be for my people."

Danny and Curtis switched on the beta cams. Lights on the cameras lit the small hut. Tika resembled a criminal in a police interrogation room. The two beams of light played over her and cast moving shadows on the leaf-walls behind her.

"Too bright?" Danny said.

"I'm fine," she said.

Halperin let out a long, loud exhale. "What did the chief say?"

"It has been going on for a few months. More so during the summer, he said. Several teenage boys have gone missing. They'd head to the river for water, or out in groups to hunt for wild pigs; only they never returned."

"Never? How many."

"Fifteen."

"Fifteen?" Halperin threw his hands up and walked away. "I don't like this."

Ignoring his boss, Rick leaned closer to Tika. "When did the last boy go missing?"

"A few days ago. He was in the forest. He went alone. He had his spear with him. Men from the tribe retrieved the spear. It was snapped in two."

Halperin let out a moan. "Seriously?"

"What does the chief think is happening?" Rick said.

"Spirits are stealing the boys. That's what Chief Amu thinks."

"And you? What do you think?"

She shook her head. "I'm not sure."

Rick knew Tika was raised by the Wairoku people. Schooling might have taught her new things, new ways to look at life, but could it ever remove tradition and beliefs she observed and practiced since birth? "Have any of them been found?"

"No. None of them.

***

Dinner was a big deal, a major production. Rick walked with his team toward a large fire. A wild pig turned on a spit over the flames. Women led them to a table. They sat on stools on either side of the Chief and his wife. Wood plates were filled with sliced bananas, garcinia, and diospyros fruits, exotic vegetables and sago palm. It was hard not to feel like royalty.

The wonderful mix of aromas assaulted Rick's nostrils. He didn't realize just how hungry he was until now. As much as he appreciated the hospitality, he was more anxious to fish the river. There was no way he would be rude and risk insulting the chief. If anything, it would be an early night, which was okay. It had been nearly two days of traveling, and the idea of getting a good night's sleep was kind of alluring.

The pig was cut into slabs and chunks of meat. The chief ensured his guests were fed first. The pig's face was severed from the carcass. The ears and cheek were considered delicacies and were set in front of Rick and his team, while the body of the pig was passed out to the other tribesmen. Rick would have gladly switched plates with anyone of them, but instead he picked at the food that had graciously been served to him. The meat was tender and nearly melted in his mouth.

The fruit was juicy and refreshing.

"What are these?" Rick said.

Tika picked a plump lump out of the bowl Rick pointed at, and popped the food into her mouth. "Capricorn," she said. "Try one."

Rick watched Tika's eyes as he ate a Capricorn. It crunched when he bit down. "Tastes a little like seasoned sunflower seeds. What is it?"

"They are the roasted larvae of Capricorn beetles harvested from fallen Sago palms."

It was too late. Rick had already swallowed the cooked larvae. If not, he would have spit it out.

"They're good, right?" Tika said, and ate another.

Rick eyed the bowl. She watched him. He ate another. "Yeah, they are."

Everything tasted amazing and, thankfully, the rain had stopped. It didn't change the fact that everything was still wet and covered in mud. Rick suspected this to be the norm and may take time to get used to.

Then came the drums, and before long, the dancing started.

Rick was not sure what they'd been served in their cups. It was a sweet tasting drink that went down smoothly. It had to contain alcohol, but he did not realize how potent it was until a native woman reached for his hand to lead him onto the earthen dance floor. His legs wobbled, and he nearly fell onto his partner. She giggled and held him up.

Looking back, Rick saw Tika clapping and laughing. Laughing at him, he imagined.

Then a catchy beat was pounded out on the drums. It was hard not to feel the rhythm from the music. Halperin was hitting the juice hard. He kept refilling his cup. Rick saw Curtis try to stop him more than once, shaking his head and placing palm over the top of the pitcher. Halperin ignored the warnings.

Danny, on the other hand, was enamored with the beat. He stood and offered a hand to Joanne. She stood and followed him toward Rick and the native woman.

It felt surreal. Rick knew his vision was somewhat obscured. He heard the drums, knew his feet were moving. He saw the others dancing, the others seated around them. He could not ignore the tall, tall trees surrounding everyone, nor could he ignore an empty pit that grew inside his gut. All he kept wondering was what his wife might be doing at home right now. That thought alone killed the moment for him. Killed it.

CHAPTER 11

There were no nets over the beds. The mosquitoes were the size of ravens. The bug spray they brought seemed useless. In fact, Danny kept saying he thought the spray attracted insects.

Brent and Rick spent the night in one bed, Danny and Curtis in another, while Joanne enjoyed a bed all to herself.

Rick was anxious to begin work. He could not think of a time when he wanted to be out fishing more than he did right now. Climbing out of bed, he felt a nausea hit his stomach and worried he might vomit. His legs were not steady. If he hadn't of seen the hut's foundation on stilts, he would have sworn the home spun. He did not remember going to bed or leaving the fire last night. He assumed he'd stumbled back with the others but couldn't say for sure. Pressing fingers against his temples, Rick silently prayed for coffee to appear magically.

He managed to open his eyes long enough to look at his wristwatch. 6:00 AM. It was time to wake the others. Rick wanted to take advantage of the entire day. They'd amassed a ton of video already. There would be enough for several episodes. Once they filled some tapes with fishing, they might have enough footage to cover the entire season. Standing by the hut's door and looking at the morning fog low on the ground and listening to the different animals talk in the jungle, Rick felt more tranquil about their trip. For some reason, things seemed better during the day. He hated to admit it, but Krantz might be on to something with this extreme fishing.

The idea of not taking a shower made Rick apprehensive. Bathing was done in the river. The Wairoku people, apparently, went down in large groups to bathe, since no one felt safe in the water. Rick wasn't sure he'd feel safe either.

Rick left the hut. As much as he wanted to start the day, he couldn't bring himself to wake the others just yet. After enough mosquito bites they'd wake on their own. The idea of walking around the village did not seem sound. He wasn't sure how far the hospitality extended. While he did not want to be mistaken for a stranger by the chief's guards, he did want to get a feel for the area. There was no denying the sense of isolation. They were literally cut off from the rest of the world. Living like this, for even a short period of time, made him think he would forget having driven a car, used a microwave oven, or watched Ted Danson on that sitcom, *Cheers*.

It wasn't a bad thing, either. Forgetting. The Wairoku have been around for centuries, have thrived and survived. What they have isn't broken. It might not be modern, but it wasn't broken. It was simple. That made it somewhat attractive.

If not for the mosquitoes.

And the missing teenagers.

And . . . whatever was in the river.

"You're up early."

Rick nearly jumped. The voice came from behind him. Tika was walking around the left side of the hut. She had a cup in her hand.

"Good morning," he said.

"Coffee?"

"You have coffee?"

She smiled. "Follow me."

He did, gladly. "It's nice to see the rain hasn't started back up."

"It's early. Give it time. It will."

Tika was not the only one awake. Most of the tribe was. Women sat by the struts of their tree-huts and worked on chores. They all talked back and forth and smiled at Rick as he and Tika walked passed.

Rick nodded and waved hello. "Everyone is so friendly."

"They like you. They liked the way you danced and sang last night."

"Sang?"

"New York, New York. You were crooning. You don't remember any of it, do you?" She laughed.

"I recall getting up to dance," he said.

"And you did. All of you did, except for your boss. He passed out early. If he gets up at all today I'll be surprised."

"What was in that juice? You know what, never mind. I don't think I even want to know."

Stones sat around a small fire. A tin kettle sat on a grate over the flames. Tika poured coffee from it into a cup. "I do have cream and sugar, if you'd like?"

"Black is fine, thank you," he said, taking the cup and smelling the coffee. He took a sip. "You won't believe me, but I was just praying for a cup of coffee."

"I wish all prayers could be that easily answered."

Rick saw one of their boat guides, Biak. He was talking with a pregnant woman whose large breasts rested flat on a swollen belly. He assumed the woman was Biak's wife. The woman kept looking over at Rick, and then her conversation became more and more heated with Biak.

"Are they arguing?"

Tika looked in the direction Rick was staring. "She does not want him to go out fishing with you today, or at all. She is telling him that the baby is almost due. If he gets killed by the creature in the river, then their child will be raised without a father. She is very upset."

"I can see that." Rick took another sip of coffee. The last thing he wanted was to disrupt the Wairoku people. "We have to find another guide."

"We can't do that," Tika said. "Biak will be humiliated. It is an honor for him to have been selected to work as a guide for you. It is not often that people from outside of the jungle visit. He is my cousin, yes, but that is not why the chief chose him. That is coincidence. If you tell him that he cannot be your guide, it will be an embarrassment to him and an insult to their chief for making a poor selection."

Tika had amazing eyes. Rick was listening to what she said. He concentrated more on her eyes, though.

"So he must continue as your guide, yes?"

"Ah, yes, of course. How can I . . . I mean, what can we do to make it better between him and his wife?"

Tika pursed her lips and watched the couple argue for a moment. "Make sure he comes home to her."

CHAPTER 12

Before venturing out on the river, Rick wanted a chance to interview Oom, the man who'd accompanied Kota to the river to fetch water on that fateful night. Since the rain had once again begun, they stood among trees under the canopy in an attempt to keep as dry as possible while they talked. Tika translated.

"I only saw a little of the fish. Its body was large. It was very big. I thought I saw a mouth filled with long, long teeth, and I swear I could hear it chomping, its teeth crushing bone," Tika repeated.

"And you went deeper into the water and tried to save your friend?" Rick said.

"You make me sound like a hero. I was too slow to save him. The fish had eaten away so many parts of his body. It took all my strength to drag him onto land," Tika translated.

Rick faced the camera, one hand resting gently on Oom's shoulder for reassurance. "We're going into the River Eilanden. Our goal is to identify the fish responsible for the attack. The Wairoku people have stayed as far away from the water as possible. That river is their main source of water. The chief told us they are currently collecting rainwater in pails for drinking, washing, and cooking. While they do receive plenty of rainfall each day, the amount collected is hardly enough to sustain a village of over one-hundred people. With any luck, we'll catch the actual creature responsible and be able to put the mind of these villagers at ease."

Biak and Prai led Rick and his team to the river. The pirogues were still tied off where they'd been left the evening before. They brought only fishing and video gear with them.

Halperin was still in bed, green. A bucket sat on the floor beside him. Tika had been correct. He was not fit to venture out on the river this morning. He promised he'd be better and ready when they went out again at night. Rick was glad, not that Halperin was sick, but simply that he wouldn't be joining them. It took some of the pressure off. Working when the boss was around was always a bit more cumbersome.

Rick, Danny, and Tika climbed into Biak's boat. Curtis and Joanne went with Prai.

"We have an idea of what we are looking for," Rick said to the cameras. Oom's vague and subjective description was not much help. Rick wouldn't admit as much but coupled with pictures of Kota's corpse, he was at least willing to surmise that if he didn't reel in a monster, no one would be satisfied. "The creature is going to have big, long teeth, and jaws with tremendous snapping power. Whatever it is that is living along these river banks, we know it has the power to take down a full grown man."

The pirogues backed away from the dock. Prai began talking.

"They want to know where you want to fish, up or down the river?" Tika said.

"I don't want to go too far. There's no need," Rick said. "The attack happened right here. Maybe if we just cut the motors and anchor near the opposite bank we can fish from there."

Tika repeated Rick's instructions. The guides nodded.

"This going to work?" Danny said.

"Why not?" Rick said.

The anchors dropped. Outboard motors were shut off. The long pirogues bobbed on the current but held steady.

"Check out the natives," he said.

Rick turned to look. At least thirty Wairoku, including the chief, were by the dock and in the tree line, staring. Rick sucked in a deep breath and swallowed it, exhaling through his nostrils. Hours could go by without as much as a nibble. "We'll see how it plays out," Rick said. "We ready?"

Danny nodded.

"I've brought my lures from America with me. Since I am not exactly sure what I am fishing for, we may have to try a variety before we find the right one that will attract *our* creature." Rick stood his fishing pole up and removed the hook from the eyelet it had been secured through. "My line is durable and able to handle a fish weighing up to around two-hundred and fifty pounds before snapping. Notice the size of the hook. It's as big as my pointer finger and thumb if I make them into a J like this." Rick showed the camera the hook alongside his hand.

Biak said something and offered Tika a box. Rick watched out of the corner of his eye as he cringed. He had explained that when filming, there was not to be any talking. Both Biak and Prai claimed to have understood.

Tika raised an eyebrow at Biak and shushed him with a finger to her lips. Rick signaled for Danny to cut, stop filming.

"What is it?" Rick said.

"Before they prepared the pig for dinner last night, Biak harvested the heart, liver, and kidneys. He cut them up for you to use as bait," she said, handing the wood box over to Rick.

Rick leaned his pole in the crux of an arm and held the box in both hands. Realizing the pig had to have been slaughtered at least twenty hours ago, and because of the heat and humidity, he opened the box reluctantly. The pungent odor was crippling. Rick swayed and closed the box.

Biak said something.

"He wants to know if you like the bait," Tika said.

Truth was, the bait would be better than his lures. "This will work. I just--tell him--I just need a minute to get used to the smell." He waved a hand back and forth under his nose and rolled his eyes toward the back of his head.

Everyone laughed.

"I wish we had have caught that on film," Rick said, opening the box a second time.

"Oh, I got it." Curtis flashed a thumbs up from where he sat on the second pirogue, his camera aimed at Rick.

With both cameras filming again, Danny focused on a close up of muscles and organs as Rick fished through box. The parts sat in a pool of thick, coagulated blood. Rick was not positive what was what as he selected a dark piece of meat. Thinking it was a liver, he stuck the barbed hook through and secured it in place as best as possible.

Rick had an audience when he fished before in derbies and for the television show, but nothing as unnerving as the natives along the banks and up in the trees.

The rain continued to fall.

Rick laid his thumb across the line in front of his reel, brought his rod out to the side careful not to stick those on his boat as the liver dangled, and cast out toward the bank.

He did not use sinkers. The weight of the hook and liver would be enough to drop the line into the river.

Now it came down to waiting.

After three hours of reeling in perch and rainbow fish, Rick was sure the audience would thin.

It didn't.

Despite the rain, Rick felt sweat drip from under his arms and behind his knees. There had been chatter, whispers and small talk. Any talking died down after the first hour and a half.

With two lines in the water, everyone simply continued to watch and wait. Fishing was meant to be peaceful and relaxing. Once Rick turned the hobby into a career, a lot of the peacefulness and relaxation evaporated.

"Got a nibble," Curtis said.

Rick set down the pole he'd been holding. Danny moved to one side so Rick could carefully lift the second pole. He held it gently, waiting to feel for a sign that a fish was toying with the bait.

He watched the line intently. He followed it from the tip of the rod to where it disappeared into the river. He waited for a tug.

Grinding his teeth in anticipation, Rick gave the reel a quarter of a crank. While the bait would barely move from where it sat at on the riverbed, it would move.

It worked.

Rick yanked up and back on the rod. "Fish on," he said.

He let the fish run. The line made a zip sound as he let out several yards. When the run stopped, Rick spun the crank, pulling back on the rod.

The fish ran again. The line unrolled off the reel.

Rick let it.

Waited.

When the fish stopped again, Rick fought him. He cranked the reel, tugging on the pole. The hook was definitely lodged in place. As long as the line didn't snap, he'd reel in something.

The give and take lasted for fifteen minutes. "My job is to tire the fish out. I let him swim off, give him plenty of line to play with and then when he stops, I start bringing him back toward the boat. Thing is, this is a big fish. He's heavy, strong. I don't know what is on the end of the line. He hasn't broken the surface of the water, so I'm reeling him in blind. It could be a bull shark, for all I know. The thing is, I'm supposed to be tiring him out, but he is doing a great job wearing me down in return. See, he fears this is a life or death battle for him. He doesn't know I just want to have a look at him, determine if he might be responsible for the river deaths and then I'm just going to release him back into the water."

The fish splashed the river surface.

"We've got a creature on the hook. You saw how it splashed. He's a fighter. A real fighter. I'm just hoping the line doesn't snap." Rick twisted his body left and right. Biak leaned over the side of the boat. He had nothing in his hands, but looked ready to grab onto the fish and yank him into the boat.

Rick cranked the reel, cutting down the amount of line available for the fish to play with. Rick hoped the fish was getting tired out. The battle had been going on for nearly an hour now. His arms felt like rubber and his shoulders ached, but he couldn't rub or massage the muscles.

The rain fell hard. Large drops plopped into the fast moving river.

Rick spun the crank. Pulled back on the rod. Spun the crank and tugged on the rod again. Over and over.

"He doesn't have much more line to get around on. His fight has gotten a little less aggressive. I can tell he's tiring out. He and I both," Rick said. He thought about it and knew drama would be essential to viewers. "The test of strength is going to come down to who holds out the longest. Way he's fighting me, I am concerned he might just win," Rick said.

Danny and Curtis filmed everything.

The fish was by the boat. It looked like Rick's rod might snap in two. Biak reached into the water.

Rick wanted to yell for him to stop.

Biak helped Rick as they hoisted a giant creature out of the water and onto the boat.

The fish filled the belly of the pirogue.

Rick gasped and fought to catch his breath. "This catfish has got to be one-twenty-five, one-fifty." Rick handed Tika one end of a tape measure and stretched it out along the top of its body. "Three-feet, four-inches long. It's a whopper of a catfish but as you can see, they have no real teeth to speak of. Catfish are bottom feeders. They dig around for food and tend to suck in their meals rather than chomp onto them the way a shark would. This is one of the largest catfish I have ever seen. Not only that, it is also one of the biggest I've ever reeled in--not out on a charter boat. She really is mammoth."

Rick knelt beside the catfish. "Will you help me get her back into the water?"

Tika translated. Biak cocked his head to the side. He replied.

Rick looked at Danny, who shrugged.

Tika said, "Biak said it would be wrong to put this fish back into the river. The village has not had any fish in weeks. They have been living on wild pig, fruits and vegetables."

Rick did not think the described diet sounded horrible. They ate very well last night. He has almost always practiced catch and release. If they wanted the catfish, he did not want to risk insulting the Wairoku chief by setting it free in the river.

"Okay, well, let's get the fish to the villagers," Rick said.

Biak called out to the villagers along the shore. They cheered, arms raised. Rick smiled at first but then gave in to laughter, sharing in the excitement of catfish for dinner.

CHAPTER 13

The region is filled with a maze of waterways. It is easy to get turned around. After dropping the catfish off to the villagers we cruised the river. Biak and Prai acted as tour guides, and Tika translated.
The River Eilanden meets up with the Becking River. Both seem to blend and cut away separately and meet up again and eventually dump into the Digoel River south of the village. The Digoel looks far much fiercer than the other two.

Rick replaced his pen. "Anyone else getting hungry?"

Everyone agreed that they were.

"After we eat, I'd like to come back out and fish some more. Maybe we anchor close to a bank but more south, away from the village a little more. That seem alright?" Rick said.

"That should be okay," Tika said.

The rain had stopped for now. Rick's clothing was still wet. He felt perpetually wet. Part of him admired the nakedness of the Indonesian people. Didn't seem worth it to wear clothes.

"Tika," Rick said. He spoke quietly. His voice could barely be heard over the hum of the boat's motor, but Tika looked at him. "In the trees to the left, there are men covered. They have weapons."

Tika must have understood. She did not turn her head to look. Instead, her eyes searched the area. "Yes. I see them."

"Those aren't your people, are they?" he said.

"No, they are not. I believe it is members of the Yakti tribe."

"Friendly?"

"If you are . . ."

"Yakti. I get it." Rick sighed. "Are we in danger?"

"Always," she said.

Rick searched her face. There was no hint of a smile. She wasn't just telling the truth. If anything, he feared she was downplaying it. "Will they attack us?"

"My guess is that right now they are curious about you and your crew and the equipment. Right now, my guess is that you scare them."

That didn't comfort Rick. "That won't last long, will it?"

She shook her head. "The Yakti are very curious people. They'll watch for a while."

Rick waited, but Tika had stopped talking.

"You think they'll watch for a while, but eventually come looking for us, try to figure out who and what we are?" he said.

"That is exactly what I. . .think."

Had she meant to say 'fear' instead of 'think'?

"And what do we do when that happens, when they work up the courage to come looking for us?"

"I do not think it's courage they search for. The Yakti are not afraid of much. They are a very aggressive and violent tribe. I would think they are merely watching and learning before approaching," she said.

Rick looked back toward the bank. The men he'd seen were gone. He looked up and down the tree line. Nothing.

The pirogues pulled alongside two other pirogues and tied off. Everyone climbed out of the canoes.

As they walked on half-buried logs back toward the village, Brent Halperin came running toward them. "Tell me you got it? That you caught the thing responsible for Kota's death. Rick, please? You've captured it on film at least. Something."

"We weren't fishing just now," Danny said.

"More like sight-seeing, dude." Curtis smiled.

"What's up?" Rick said.

"Joanne, did you know anything about this?" Halperin said.

"About what? You haven't told us anything," Joanne said.

"Brent, what is going on?" Rick said.

"You're not going to believe this. You will never guess who else is here in this jungle with us."

"It's the whole Catch and Release crew!"

Rick looked over Halperin's shoulder. He recognized the voice. He couldn't place it. Must have had something do with being in the jungle. It felt out of place, like seeing your postal carrier grocery shopping --you recognize them, but can't recall from where.

"Rick Stone!"

That did it. Rick knew. It came like a slap across the face. "Lance Crowley," Rick said. It wasn't meant as a greeting, just a fact. A statement made out loud.

Crowley held out his arms. Rick almost laughed. Was he expecting a hug?

"What are you doing here?" Rick said.

"They heard about the body," Halperin said. "Or more specifically, they caught wind that we were coming down to film an extreme fishing show."

Crowley held out his hand. Rick did shake it. The gesture was more of an autopilot thing while still in shock.

"I brought my whole 'Casting with Lance Crowley' team too," he said. "They're chatting it up with the chief. Looks like we're going to have huts near each other. Ours is a little higher up than yours is. More like the Wairoku, but I don't think that really means anything. Do you?"

Rick looked at Tika. He wanted answers even though he knew she couldn't provide them. He spun and looked at his cameramen and Joanne, then at Biak and Prai, and finally his eyes fell on Halperin. "We should talk," he said.

"I agree," Halperin said.

"Our hut?"

"Perfect."

"Lance, if you'll excuse us?" Rick said.

"Sure, of course. Not a problem. We'll see you at dinner. I hear you guys did a fine job catching some catfish?" Crowley said.

It sounded like a dig. They *had* done a fine job catching a catfish. A huge catfish. It should feed a lot of the tribe. Most of the village, and yet because Lance Crowley said it the way he said it, with that. . .voice of his, Rick thought it was a dig, a slam.

***

"How did this happen?" Rick said. He paced back and forth. He knew his shoes tracked mud. He wasn't worried about wet dirt right now. There were more important things to be worried about.

"He didn't say," Halperin said. "He just showed up here on boats just like we did yesterday."

Casting with Lance Crowley. Catch & Release with Rick Stone. Both on scene in Indonesia. Both on the hunt for a creature swimming the freshwater rivers. "Now we're not just searching, we're racing. First one to identify the fish responsible is going to win. This whole trip could be for nothing," Rick said, and ran his hand through his hair. "Do you think he was mailed a letter, too?"

Both after the same thing. Here in Indonesia to find the creature responsible for Kota's death. It didn't matter that Rick and his crew had a day on them. They'd found nothing. Aside from capturing some great footage, the only fish they'd caught so far was cooking over a flame for dinner. The catfish's size might wow television viewers, but it wasn't the promised monster.

"It doesn't matter how he found out. Could be a mole at our network, who knows? It's not important right now. It will get handled," Halperin said. "We will find out, but right now, it's like you said. It is a race. He's turned it into a bloody competition."

"I want to get back out on the river," Rick said.

"That's a good idea," Halperin said.

"But we're going to eat first?" Danny said. He sat on a bed. His camera was on the floor between his feet.

Rick walked out of the hut, Tika right behind him.

***

"Mr. Stone? Mr.--Rick?"

Rick stopped walking and turned around. Tika pursed her lips and crossed her arms over her chest.

"I don't think I understand what is happening," Tika said.

The rain, for once, came down lightly. Like a mist. Rick was aware of the smell of everything green: the weeds and tall grass, the leaves and moss. The dense humidity seemed to slow cook it all.

"That other man and his film crew are here to fish for the creature that killed Kota," he said. He took steps toward her. He was annoyed by the rain that rolled down his forehead and into his eyes. He knew he'd never grow used to the thick heat or the perpetual wetness. Wiping away rain from his eyes with his sleeve was as pointless as carrying a towel to dry his hair.

"Why would that be bad? The chief tried to get authorities here to investigate the matter and no one came. No one would listen. As far as the Indonesian government is concerned, they want this half of the island without any of the responsibility that goes with governing the people."

"I am not against helping your chief, but this man, his crew, they are to my team what the Yakti are your people."

She cocked her head to one side. "I do not think you mean that."

Rick sighed. "No. I don't mean that, not figuratively, but metaphorically. Lance Crowley has a TV show similar to mine back in the states. If he finds the fish responsible for the attack before my team, he wins."

"Wins?"

"His network wins. His show wins. I'll be out of a job."

Tika dropped her arms to her side. "I understand."

She walked past Rick.

"Tika. Tika?"

She spun around. "I knew film crews were coming. I thought it was more to document catching the monster from the river. I knew you had a television show and that you planned to use the footage on that show, but I didn't think this was a game. I thought all of you were here doing this because you cared."

"I do care. We care," Rick said. He took an internal inventory. He had not shown a single sign of empathy. Tika had no reason to believe him.

"If the Yakti were to catch you wandering alone in the forest, they would probably hang you from a tree branch by your feet.

This lets all the blood drain from your body and pool in your head. They would slide a bucket under you and cut your throat. When you bled out, they would peel your skin off your bones. They wouldn't throw it away. Human leather is durable and has many uses. After they cut you down, the Yakti will ram a spit through your ass, up and out of your mouth. They'd stick you over a fire and cook you until a nice golden--"

"I get it, Tika. I said I was sorry."

"No," she said. "You didn't."

"I'm sorry."

"And Kota?"

"I want to find the fish responsible for his death, not just for my show, but so the Wairoku can at the very least learn more about what they are up against in their rivers. We probably will never catch the actual fish. If we can at least figure out the species likely to have attacked Kota, then we'll have accomplished the goal." Rick knew everything he said, he'd meant sincerely.

CHAPTER 14

Chief Amu looked like a man who had just won millions. The smile he wore revealed the sentiment, along with the puffed out chest and animated gestures and tone of voice when he spoke.

"The chief is excited to have so many people here helping him," Tika said to Rick and his team.

Danny and Curtis had been given direction. They were to film everything but avoid at all costs catching Lance or his team in any frames.

The meal was catfish tonight, not wild pig. Aside from the entree, everything matched the meal from the night before. There were full bowls of fruits and vegetables, filled cups of a natural alcoholic beverage, and that Halperin stayed far, far away from it.

There was drumming, singing and dancing.

Lance carefully made his way toward Rick and Tika with a full drink in his hand, and sat down between them. "This is quite a shindig."

"It is."

"They do this when you first got here?"

"They did."

"I was told this place was going to be hot and wet, but man, I had no idea just how hot and wet it really would be."

Rick popped a slice of garcinia into his mouth. The flavor exploded on his tongue. He almost closed his eyes to savor the moment. Lance ruined it with the sound of his voice.

"What? Not even a two word reply to the heat and humidity?"

"It is hot and wet here."

Lance snickered. His eyes locked onto Rick. He laughed. He rocked back and forth, as he laughed a little more. "You really do hate me, don't you?"

"Hate you? Why would I hate you, Lance. I don't even know you." It was true. The two had met at several fishing derbies.

They'd even gone for beers a time or two. Things changed when Lance was offered a fishing show, stealing Rick's format, with a competing network.

"You could have fooled me. You know what, though? I don't blame you. If I were you, I'd hate me, too."

Rick couldn't help but stare at Lance. "You would hate you too, if you were me?"

"I would, absolutely."

"And why is that?"

"Lots of reasons," Lance said.

"Because you are a cheat and a thief?"

"I am, among other things."

Rick clapped a hand onto Lance's leg as he stood up. "Have some more to drink. I have no idea what is in there, but it is delicious. If you'll excuse me."

Lance drank from his cup. "Night fishing?"

Rick just stared at Lance.

"You don't have any worries. My team's tired. We're not going out tonight. We're headed right to bed. All those flights, you'd think we'd be well rested. I feel like I've been sleepless the last two days." He sipped more drink. "Maybe because I have been. Hey, good luck out there. Hope you catch some. . .stuff."

Rick shook his head. He and Tika walked over to where the chief sat, enjoying the dancers before him. "Chief, it was another amazing meal. Thank you for your hospitality. If you will forgive us, my team and I would like to go out fishing. We do not want to waste anymore time trying to catch the creature living in your river."

Tika translated.

Chief Amu nodded as he stood and bowed slightly. Rick bowed in return, then turned and waved for his team to follow him. Curtis was the only one who looked disappointed. He seemed to have his eyes on one of the natives. The young woman was topless and danced directly in front of Curtis as if for his exclusive pleasure.

"Curtis," Rick said, "come on. Let's go. Curtis!"

"Coming, Rick. I'm coming."

***

Rick imagined the view from up in the surrounding mountains as breathtaking. The sky at dusk over such a dense forest must look amazing. From under the canopy and beneath the falling rain, it was impossible to gauge how anything really looked other than dark and green.

The sounds were intense. The animals that slept nights missed out on the nightlife in the jungle.

They were roughly a hundred miles north of the Arafura Sea, and beyond that, Australia. Rick always wanted to visit the land down under. If time permitted, maybe he'd extend work into a mini-vacation and see some of the sights. He realized two things. He was enjoying time away from home, with the exception of missing his son, and he was in no hurry to confront his wife. The conversation couldn't end well. The idea of divorce frightened him. It was not something he believed in. He saw no way of keeping a marriage alive if she was unfaithful.

"Rick?"

"Yes?"

Tika offered a gentle smile, her lips just slightly curling up. It was as if she understood he had been mentally elsewhere, his mind on personal thoughts that threatened any concentration. "Biak said we could head north up the river, stay along the banks, and see what happens."

"That sounds perfect. Our lighting good?" Rick pointed at Danny.

"Check."

"Curtis?"

Curtis switched on a light. "Check."

"Then let's do this," Rick said, and clapped his hands.

Biak and Prai started the outboard motors. The team piled into the pirogues. The boats had become like beds. Each person had their side. Rick, Danny, and Tika road with Biak, while Halperin, Joanne, and Curtis stayed with Prai.

With the cameras on him, Rick spoke to a yet-to-be-determined audience. "There is a perception in the states that when it is nighttime, it is dark out. Trust me. In the states, we have no idea what darkness is. There are clouds in the sky right now. They covered the stars and the moon from our view. It is pitch black on this river. Pitch black. The predators in the area must either have exceptional cat-like eyesight or hunt using their other senses. If it weren't for the camera lights none of us would be able to see our hands in front of our faces."

Rick's shirt stuck to his body. He knew he'd not showered that morning. With the constant rain and thick humidity, it almost didn't make sense. The natives didn't have running water. They washed in the river. With the unknown fish threatening, bathing had become less important to the general population. He knew he smelled raw. This became obvious when his nose refused to stop wrinkling when near Danny.

The box with pig parts still sat in the pirogue. Rick readied his rod, used his knife to cut away a chunk of meat, and fed the barbed hook through the muscle. "I am going to use pig heart to fish for our creature. It's a good size piece of bait and should attract hungry predators. Don't forget, Koto was attacked and killed at dusk. That leads me to believe that the fish responsible feeds at night. We're just a few hundred yards north of the Wairoku village. We're going to keep lighting to a minimum. We don't want that change in environment to cause the fish to be suspicious of their surroundings."

Biak steered the pirogue toward the bank and shut the outboard motor. He dropped an anchor into the river. It caught on the bottom. The river pulled at the boat taking it south until the anchor pulled tight. Biak told Tika they were ready.

Rick stood at the front of the pirogue. He set one foot on the edge as he cast his line toward the opposite bank. "I am excited to fish at night in Papua. I've never done anything like this. There is no denying the rush I'm getting. I can feel my hands shaking. I could be a little nervous, too, but mostly it's just pure excitement. I guess it would be similar to someone going from bow hunting deer in November in New York, to rifle hunting lions in the Serengeti as part of some exotic safari. It's too dark to see them, but my arms are covered in goose bumps. You're just going to have to take my word on that."

On the bank behind Rick something rustled leaves, and a branch snapped. Rick spun his head around, his eyes strained to see into the black night to no avail. "Danny, film the woods."

"I heard it, too," Danny said.

The camera light hit the riverbank like a weak spotlight. The beam of light barely penetrated the darkness. It was just strong enough to make shadows move. Danny panned left and right. Large leaves were about all that was visible.

"It could have been anything," Tika said.

"My point exactly," Rick said. Aside from feeling excited about fishing on a foreign river at night, there was some fear mixed in. Plenty of fear, if Rick was honest.

"I don't think we should be shining the light into the trees," Tika said.

Rick wanted to ask why, but thought he might already know the answer. He concentrated on reeling in his bait. He checked the hook. The heart was still affixed in place. He re-cast. He knew he should be talking to the camera, reporting on his thoughts and progress--or lack thereof. Unnerved, he just stared at the line, as much of it as he could see in the little light allowed.

"Shh. What's that?" It was Joanne. Their pirogue had continued to go north and then south filming Rick from different angles while he fished. At some point the canoe had pulled up alongside them.

"What?" Rick said. He strained to listen, closing his eyes. "I don't--"

"Shh," she said.

"Tika, have Prai kill his motor," Rick said.

Both Pirogues sat silent on the river.

Rick held a finger to his lips, as he listened.

Then he heard distinctly what Joanne heard. . .

CHAPTER 15

"It's another boat," Joanne said.

Baik and Tika conversed. Tika said, "It's coming from the village."

Rick shook his head. He set his rod down. His weight shifted. The boat rocked side to side. "That son of a--"

"We don't know it's him," Halperin said, and held tight to both sides of the pirogue. "Can you sit down? I'm not in any mood to fall into that river. Not with whatever it is that's in there, and certainly not at night."

"You think it's Lance?" Joanne said. "It would be just like him."

The stared into the darkness and listened as the hum of an outboard motor became louder.

Rick said. "Don't stop filming."

Rick saw a penlight-sized beam round the bend. The size of the light grew, and then doubled. The chugging of two motors became louder and louder.

"It's him," Joanne said. "He told me he and his crew were exhausted from the trip here, and that they'd be turning in early."

"Told me the same thing," Rick said. "Probably got all worked up when he saw us take off. If we catch this fish before him, his entire trip was for nothing."

"Works both ways," Halperin said.

"And you know what? He's scaring the fish. We're not going to catch a thing with those rickety motors. They'll scare away anything with gills. We might as well pack it in. Go back and call it a night," Rick said, his arms flailing.

"We're giving up?" Joanne said.

"No," Rick said, "that was sarcasm. I'll stay out all night fishing. I have no problem with that. He's not going to show up here and steal this from us. There's no way I am giving up that easily."

He waited until the boats got closer. He thought for sure, when Lance's team noticed them, they'd avoid Rick and his group. Instead, the two pirogues headed directly toward them.

"Is he out of his mind?" Halperin said.

"Maybe he thinks he's going to cast alongside of us?" Curtis said, and chuckled.

Rick cupped his hands by his mouth. "Hey, Lance! What in the world do you think you're doing? We were here first."

It started in Rick's gut. He placed a hand across his stomach. Maybe it was the catfish or the citrus fruits for dinner, but Rick didn't think so. He felt acid bubble in his belly. It was because of Lance. At least *one* of the causes for the pain he blamed on Lance.

The motors on the approaching pirogues shut off simultaneously. The boats drifted closer. The guides used paddles and angled into perfect positions. All four pirogues sat side by side. Rick watched Biak and Prai greet the other two guides.

"I mean, Lance, come on. What the hell are you doing? You're going to fish here? Right here? Really?" Rick was ready to leap from one boat into the next. His fingers rolled into his palms. His fists were so tight his knuckles looked white. There were now four cameras filming everything.

Lance huffed, as if out of breath. "Rick, tThe chief sent me. We need you back at the village."

Rick looked at Tika. "The chief?"

"Three kids, Rick. They're missing," Lance said.

The four guides and Tika talked at once. They talked fast and loud. They used their hands and body gestures.

"He is right," Tika said. "We need to get back. The chief is organizing a search party."

***

It seemed like forever getting back to the village. Lance and his pirogues went first while Rick's team pulled up anchors. The camera lights played on the river, illuminating low hanging tree branches. The moving shadows constantly distracted. Rick was looking left and right, ahead and behind, certain that all of them were, if not being stalked, then at least watched.

The boats glided up to the small dock and tied off. Halperin stepped off his pirogue before anyone else.

The cameras shined lights on what appeared to be the entire tribe. They were gathered together and many held lit torches. The rain didn't put out the flames which led Rick to believe the cloth, or the wicks were soaked in some type flammable agent.

The chief, despite his youth, looked old. Running a village must put wear on a person. "Tika, can we find out what happened? Can you talk to the chief?"

Two women stood by Chief Amu. They cried. Young kids clung to their bare legs. One woman carried a baby in a papoose slung over her shoulder. The infant was latched onto a nipple and sucked greedily.

Tika strode toward her people. She walked with confidence and purpose. Until now, *this moment*, Rick had not been able to imagine Tika as a Wairoku. He'd merely thought of her as a well-educated woman who spoke fluent *Bahasa*.

Danny sidled up next to Rick and lowered his camera. "I am not liking this, boss. Not one bit. It's been one creepy thing after another here. I think in the morning we just head home. Collect some unemployment for the winter and worry about jobs in the spring."

Rick gritted his teeth. "Turn that camera back on. Zoom in on Tika and the chief. Where's Curtis? Curtis!"

"Right here," Curtis said.

"Why aren't you filming?" Rick said.

"This has absolutely nothing to do with fishing."

Danny clapped Curtis on the back of the head. "Think bigger, man. We have some rare footage here. There's no telling what's going to happen. Catch and Release can use some of it, and we'll get paid, but how about National Geographic? Wild America? We could be set for life!"

Halperin cleared his throat. "The film is property of the network, I'm afraid. You'll get credit for shooting whatever it is that ends up getting shot. That I can promise you."

"Credit?"

Halperin bit down on his upper lip. "Bonuses, too."

"How about a fair percentage. I'm thinking ten each," Danny said. "That's amazingly fair."

"How about we talk about this later?" Halperin said.

Danny raised his eyebrows. "I'm not filming a single thing. Curtis put your camera down."

"I wasn't filming."

"Five percent each, but I will still have to clear it with the network."

"Ten. Five is an insult, and when I say ten, it's across the board. Royalties on anything and everything. When it airs, whatever gets published. Betamax. VHS. Sales, rentals. Across the board, Halperin. Do we have a deal?"

"I think we really need to discuss this later."

Danny and Curtis just stood there. Quiet. Eyes on Halperin. Rick admired their stand.

"Fine. Okay? Fine. Ten percent."

"Each. Ten for Curtis. Ten for me."

"That is an absurd amount."

"Each." Danny was not going to budge. That much was clear.

"Ten percent. Each. Agreed. Now film. Everything."

Biak tapped Rick on the shoulder. He talked fast. Rick wanted to understand the man. He felt like he should understand everything said. "I don't know what you are saying."

Biak motioned with his hand. He made a gesture over his belly, exaggerating the stomach, as if pregnant. "Your wife. You want to check on your wife. Go, go and check on her," Rick said.

Joanne took small steps without leaving from her spot. Her feet just kept moving. She watched everything unfolding around her.

"You alright?" Rick walked closer to her.

"Can I tell you something?"

"Of course."

"I know what is coming next. I just want to go home. I don't want to be here anymore. I feel it. I can just feel it, Rick. Something is wrong here. Something is terribly wrong."

CHAPTER 16

"What's going on here, Rick. I mean, besides some monster of a fish in their river?" Lance Crowley was poised for his cameramen. There was nothing sincere about the question.

Rick thought he looked like he was acting, badly, which just made it worse. "You know as much as we do at this point. In fact you came and got us for help. Not the other way around, so maybe I should be asking you.

"Cut," Lance said. "Jerry, Tyson, quit it. Cut."

The camera lights went off.

"Okay, you and me, Rick. What gives?"

"I already told you. I have no clue. The chief mentioned something when we first got here about people going missing. I honestly just thought he meant drowning." Rick shrugged, looked to Joanne for confirmation of the conversation.

"He thought we weren't here just to fish," Joanne said.

"And you are?" Lance said.

"I'm the director, Joanne Wagner. This is Danny and Curtis. I believe you already know Brent Halperin."

Lance and Rick had competed for the lead on Catch & Release. Neither angler knew it, though. The network interviewed both and eventually chose Rick Stone. Didn't take long before Lance was picked up by a different producer.

"These are my cameramen: Tyson McFadden, Jerry Hendrickson. And my director, Albert Lincoln, he is over with our guide trying to get more details," Lance said.

Everyone shook hands.

"This is a search party, I'm guessing," Tyson said.

Joanne shivered.

Rick just stared. He wanted to comfort her. There was just no way to do it without feeling awkward. They weren't close. If anything, Halperin and she hit it off. Halperin looked more ruffled, as if *he* needed a hug. He stood with his left arm across his belly, his right elbow on his left wrist, his hand to his mouth and his thumbnail being chewed off. "What do you mean by a search party?"

"Here comes Tika," Rick said. "She'll be able to tell us exactly what's happening. Then we won't have to stand out here guessing in the rain."

They all huddled close. Four cameras were on. It was overkill. Rick wanted to tell everyone to quit it, to give it a rest. There was no way he could. It was part of the job. And after watching the percentage bickering wars, he knew his request would be futile. He'd never have to remind his men to film again.

"What did you find out?" Rick said.

"Three people are missing: a brother and sister, and another boy. The boys were both eleven, and the girl, ten."

Twelve was the age when most of the girls in the village married. It was not good if she was still single by fourteen. If a teenager made it until sixteen and was still not married, the entire family shared in the shame. There was no punishment, no public humiliation, the shame was simply assumed.

"And it happened by the river?" Rick said.

Tika shook her head. She pointed in the opposite direction of the water. "No, they were in the woods. We're going to search for them."

"How long have they been gone?" Joanne's tone of voice possessed an audible tremble.

"Since before dinner."

"Is that common."

"No, not at nighttime, and not with what's been going on lately. It isn't that Chief Amu instituted a curfew, but it was generally expected that everyone stay close to the village."

"Generally expected?" Lance shook his head.

"They're kids," Rick said, as if that explained everything.

"What's that mean?"

"Kids here are no different than kids at home. Best time to explore is when you are not allowed to," Rick said.

"What's next? What is everyone going to do?" Joanne said.

"We're going into the woods to find them," Tika said.

Rick looked over at the pirogues. He wanted to fish. It was late. He was actually still feeling very tired and worn out.

"Does the chief want our help?" Rick said, asking the question he knew everyone was thinking.

Tika said, "You don't have to help if you don't want to."

It was not what Rick wanted to hear. Tika's response was vague. A yes or a no. Cut and dry. Rick felt torn. He did not drop his gaze, but kept his eyes locked on Tika's. He worried if he looked around he'd be able to read yes and no answers on the faces of his team. He did not want his reply to be influenced, but neither did he plan to answer on behalf of everyone. They would each have to make their own decision. "I'm going to help you."

"It's not me you are agreeing to help." Tika made her point with the sharp edge along the tone of her voice.

"What about us?" Joanne said.

Rick shook his head. "That's up to you. I have no idea what's out in that jungle or any clue as to what's going on. I can't make that call for you. You each have to."

Danny lifted his camera. "I'm with you, boss."

"Me, too," Curtis said.

Rick didn't think it had to do with simply capturing rare footage. It could be. It might be about the money. Rick didn't want to believe that. Just like he wanted to believe his choice had nothing to do with Tika.

Joanne and Halperin stayed silent. It clearly was not a yes, but neither was it a no. It was, however, an answer.

"What do we do?" Rick said, finally.

"We're going to split up into groups and search areas around the village working our way out until we come across something that points us in the right direction." Tika was in control now. She seemed to know it. This was no longer some job of her translating.

They were now about to embark on a search and rescue.

CHAPTER 17

From where Rick stood among the gathered Wairoku, he watched the interaction between Biak and his wife. He wished he could hear and understand the conversation between them. It wasn't so he could be nosy, but his curiosity was like a hunger within him. The communication between him and Karen was so poor and ineffective that he wondered how couples on the opposite side of the globe handled relationships.

Far from the perfect husband, Rick knew his ability to share feelings, thoughts, and ideas lacked. It was never Karen's fault that he was inadequate at verbalizing anything other than fishing talk. However, he wished she had at least taken some time to encourage him to open up. She never did. Any attempt made felt forced and unnatural. It was almost as if she really didn't care about how he felt, or what he thought.

Then there was Jared.

Rick watched Biak rub his wife's swollen belly. He practically saw the love waft off the palm of the man's hand with each gentle and sincere pass.

Jared would suffer the most if after this trip Rick asked for a divorce.

Divorce might not be the answer. This far away from home, though, he just couldn't envision any other solutions.

Someone whistled. Loud. Long.

Biak kissed his wife and then ran toward everyone else. He stood next to Rick and offered up a nod. Rick nodded in return. It seemed like an acknowledgement passed between them.

Danny returned from their hut. He'd fetched fresh batteries and blank tapes for the cameras. While torches served a purpose, no one denied camera lights would pierce the darkness more effectively.

Tika said, "The chief would like one of your camera men to go with his group."

"I'll do it," Curtis said. "I'll go with him."

Rick grimaced. He really didn't want the team split up. It was bad enough that Joanne and Halperin were staying behind. At least with them, Rick felt confident that they'd be safe. These were adults. Ultimately not his responsibility. It didn't change the fact that he actually felt responsible, regardless. "I need you to be sure about this, Curtis."

"I am."

"You won't even know what anyone is saying." There was no way Tika wasn't staying with him. He couldn't imagine going on this search without her.

"Look, dude, it's easy. I find two or three kids, and all I have to do is point. They look where I'm pointing, and it's over. Same goes the other way. I see them all of a sudden start running, it isn't like I need to know what their running from. I just start running, too. Right? Dude, it can't be more basic than that."

It can't be more basic, Rick thought. It certainly could become more complicated, and get more complicated fast. There were far too many variables to even consider alternate problems that might arise. The chance that everything played out smoothly seemed unlikely.

"I'll be good, dude. Promise." Curtis clapped Rick on the back. To Tika he said, "We're going to find these missing kids. They're going to be all right. I know it."

Tika thanked him.

He jogged toward another group of Wairoku. Rick's mouth felt terribly dry, his tongue thick. The rainwater rolling down his face and onto his lips did nothing to help.

"Are you ready? We're about to start looking," Tika said.

Rick nodded.

Danny lifted his camera. "You good, boss?"

"Of course. All good."

"Well, let's do this. And, rolling."

***

Rick imagined machetes would work wonders slicing a path through the dense woods. The knife on his hip would be more of a hindrance than anything. He and Danny seemed to be the only ones struggling. Even Tika moved swiftly. The ground was made of thick mud. Fallen trees were slick with wet moss. The ground growth was determined to snag a foot, perfect to cause tripping and falls.

"Not sure how great this footage is going to come out. It's hand-shaky, let me tell you. No one is going pay money to watch something filmed in the dark on a hand-held camera, where all I am doing is shaking the lens as I move through darkness. It will never sell," Danny said.

"Just keep filming," Rick said.

"I haven't stopped. I'm just sayin', is all."

"We're falling behind, too."

"Less talking, more walking."

"You see how fat I am? This heat, the humidity, a hike through the forest; I'm doing the best I can, boss. Best I can."

"I know you're not complaining," Rick said.

"Oh, but I am."

Rick stopped. "Then you should have stayed back with Joanne and Halperin."

Danny lowered the camera and stopped walking, too. He stood up straight. The sound of the large raindrops pummeling strong green leaves was constant. "Why are you yelling at me? I'm out here, same as you. Looking for these missing kids."

"I'm sorry," Rick said. "It wasn't supposed to go like this. Any of it. None of this."

"That's kind of the beauty of it, boss. We're on a literal adventure. A once-in-a-lifetime thing here. It's about more than the show, don't you see that? This, when you think about it, it's surreal."

"Why have you stopped?" Tika stood on a fallen tree limb, one hand held a lit torch, the other palm-pressed against peeled bark. She looked nothing like a native Wairoku, as much as she resembled a female version of Spielberg's newest character, Indiana Jones, from that movie about a treasure-hunting archaeologist. "You fall too far behind, and you can easily get turned around in these woods. Once that happens, you're lost. Only then, we're not searching for three missing children and two adults. We're still just searching for the missing children. Do you understand me?"

"I do," Rick said. "We're right behind you."

Tika stared at them for a moment before turning and almost immediately disappearing back into the foliage.

"Okay, I am not going to lie," Danny said, "but that was hot."

Thunder boomed. The *roll* echoed as it passed over the rain forest canopy. "It can't possibly rain more, can it?" Rick said as he stepped over the limb Tika had been standing on only moments ago.

"I think it *can*. I suspect it is about to," Danny said, right behind Rick.

***

With each step Rick took he sank in the mud. He pulled his legs to break free from undergrowth that reached for, and grabbed at, and latched onto his feet. The continued entanglement frustrated him and was tiring. His clothing dripped with rain mixed with sweat. He huffed on thick air that filled and seemed to clog his lungs.

"I don't see any light, Rick. Nothing." Danny stopped walking. He pointed the camera at the ground. The circumference of light was focused on a single patch of grass like weeds.

Rick looked around. Danny was right, especially with the camera light gone. They appeared to be alone. Aside from Danny's heavy breathing and his own, Rick heard only the rain. Total darkness surrounded them. "Raise the camera," Rick said.

"I can't. I just can't do it. My arms feel like rubber. I think my side is going to split. How long have we been out here? We don't even know if we've been following everyone or just wandering around aimlessly." Danny coughed and spit into the weeds.

Rick stood next to his friend. He squatted next to the camera light and checked his watch. "It's almost eleven. We've been out here over an hour."

"And how long since we've seen Tika?"

"I don't know. Fifteen, twenty minutes." Rick looked left and right and left again. His eyes could not pierce the darkness. He saw nothing, not trees, branches or shadows. "Give me the camera."

Rick used the recorder like a flashlight. "I think the river is that way."

"You sure? I'd swear it's to our right."

Rick bit into his upper lip. He didn't want to admit it, but Danny could be right.

Something rustled in the leaves.

"What was that?" They both said.

Rick trained the light toward where the sound had emerged and panned around some, only *sort* of hoping to find whatever it was moving in the thicket.

"What was it?"

"I don't see anything," Rick said.

"Should we try to go back? Tika said it. If we get lost, we're on our own. The priority is the kids. Not finding us."

She had said that. "We turn around and try heading back, we could wind up more lost."

"More lost than if we just keep going forward?"

Rick didn't have an answer. "We can't just stay right here."

"But maybe we should," Danny said. "When I was a kid we'd all go to the mall or something. My mother used to tell my brothers and me that if we got separated not to go looking for her but to stay put, and she'd find us."

Rick laughed. "My mother said the same thing. Or to go up to a woman who had kids. She felt another mother would be less likely to harm or kidnap someone else's kid."

"Exactly, and since I don't see any moms with kids around, maybe we should just stay where we are. This rainforest is the Wairoku backyard. Let them look for their kids. They'll come for us. Sooner or later, someone will come looking for us."

Rick squatted next to Danny, again. "That just might make the most sense. I'm just worried that--"

Leaves rustled. A branch snapped.

"We're not alone," Danny said. His words were barely audible over the sound of rainfall.

Rick went to lift the camera.

Danny clapped a hand onto Rick's wrist. "Shut the light."

"We can't see anything then."

"You're giving away our position. Whatever is out there, it knows right where we are," Danny said.

"What if it's Tika?"

"Would she be sneaking up on us? If it's her, where's her torch?"

Rick fumbled with the camera, looking for the off switch.

The light swiveled upward, and before the beam extinguished it showe on a horrid face.

A large, wet snout. Short, sharp tusks. There was a snort.

Plunged into darkness, Rick wasn't sure if it was him or Danny, but someone screamed.

CHAPTER 18

The wild pig snorted. Rick thought something happened to his legs. They felt cemented in place.

"Do we run?"

Rick didn't know the right thing to do. Pigs were huge and dangerous. With a bear, one was supposed to play dead. He spoke, teeth set, lips barely twitched. "Don't move."

The pig snorted again. It stepped closer to them. Rick swore, despite the rain, he felt breath and spittle spray his face. He imaged a giant snout by his forehead; sharp tusks poised a fraction of an inch from thrusting into his flesh.

Everything inside him screamed to turn and bolt.

The pigs ran fast. Size did not slow them down once running. He knew this much to be true.

If the thing chased them, it would win.

He figured they'd wandered into its lair. Maybe it protected baby piglets close to its home. Regardless of why, it was letting them know they were not welcome.

For whatever reason, the wild pig had not attacked. It made noise, as if wanting them to know *it* knew they were there.

Rick remembered the knife. He brought his hand to the sheath. He curled his hand over the handle and drew the blade. He'd never killed an animal on purpose.

There was once on a weekend getaway in the Thousand Islands with his cousins. They had a BB gun. Behind the cottage by the water, they took turns firing at a flock of birds perched on a utility wire. Ravens. His older cousin wanted him to try, gave the small rifle a pump and handed it off. Rick took it reluctantly. He knew he'd have to fire the gun whether he wanted to or not. He aimed the barrel at the birds and closed an eye. Even at seven, he knew his chance of actually hitting a bird was slim to none. He wanted to *not* aim and to miss on purpose. When he fired the BB hit a raven fell and it dropped off the wire and fell to the ground. They ran to see it, certain it was dead. The raven's eyes were wide open and one wing fluttered. "It's not dead," his cousin said. "We have to shoot it again." Rick wanted to close his eyes then. They shot several BBs into the raven before it finally surrendered and died. It had been horrible, something he'd never forget.

"Rick?"

"What?"

"What do we do?"

Not talk was what flashed first through Rick's mind. "We have to move. It wants us to leave."

The pig snorted, as if it agreed.

"Slow, though. No sudden moves."

It was far too dark to see anything. Rick assumed Danny was moving away from the pig, as well. Rick took a tentative step backwards, and then another.

The beast had been between them. He didn't want to become separated from Danny. They would just have to meet up somewhere else. Where? He had no idea. Getting away from the animal was the main priority at the moment.

A twig snapped. Danny screamed. More branches cracked under the weight of something on the run. At first Rick thought the pig was after Danny.

Feet from him, the pig snorted and then gave chase. Its weight caused the ground to shake. Fallen branches crunched. There was no mistaking the different sounds now.

Rick turned and ran, blindly.

He couldn't be sure if the pig was after him or Danny. He wasn't going to stand still long enough to find out. His hand slapped a tree, and he went around it, hopefully out of the direct path of the pig. He had no idea if they could see in the dark. He knew he could not. He continued to run. He stepped as best he could.

When he tripped, his hands shooting out in front of him to break the fall, he cringed, eyes squeezing tightly shut. He waited to be trampled on. He envisioned sharp tusks stabbing into his back.

It didn't happen. He got to his feet.

The pig had to be chasing Danny.

The darkness was too complete.

Rick started forward. It was hard not to start running again. It took a certain discipline to walk slowly and step carefully.

He listened for Danny, and for sounds from anyone, from anywhere. He could not even hear the river. He was lost. Again, he used restraint to keep from calling out for help. The Wairoku people must be around. The tribe had flooded the forest.

Where was Tika?

Hairs on the back of his neck rose on end. Rick was sure something was out there watching him, stalking him. His mind remembered the natives he'd seen along the river bank. Potentially dangerous and hostile. Where was their village? Could he be walking toward it? How would they react if he suddenly appeared?

"Hello?" He could not hold it in anymore. Fear filled him. "Hello!"

***

Rick held his knife in a white-knuckle grip. He decided to climb a tree. Standing in the thicket made him uneasy. The wild pig could return, or it could be a different one altogether. If violent natives, enemies of the Wairoku came looking for him, he didn't want to just be standing out in the open. He straddled a thick branch, hugged the trunk, and held his knife.

He almost laughed at how tired he felt. He kept yawning. Rick wondered if his body was just trying to shut down. A defense mechanism against dealing with everything going on. He had no idea what time it was. The only thing he knew for sure was that there were still far too many hours until sunrise.

There had not been nearly enough time to research this land before heading across the ocean. If there were snakes coiled nearby, he'd just assume they were venomous, with huge fangs.

Something was below him. He heard it. It breathed in and out. In and out. He hugged the tree tighter.

Tempted to yell out a hello again, Rick decided against it and kept quiet. He had no idea what waited below.

He closed his eyes. He couldn't see anything anyway.

He waited.

And waited, suddenly worried he might yawn again. What a way to reveal where you are hiding. A yawn.

That thought almost made him laugh.

He added it. A yawn. A laugh.

Both horrible ways to be found out.

He needed to clear his mind. He worried he might be losing it. He had never felt this kind of fear. He thought it might be like treading water in an ocean during the night and knowing it was just a matter of time before a shark came up and chunked away his lower half.

CHAPTER 19

"There he is!"

Joanne ran at Rick as he stepped out of the forest. She wrapped her arms around him. "I'm okay," he said, "just thirsty."

"We were so worried about you," she said. "Where's Danny?"

Rick looked over Joanne's shoulder. He saw Curtis, Brent, and Tika. "What? He didn't come back?"

"He was with you, wasn't he?" Joanne pulled out of the hug. She walked past Rick to edge of the forest. She stuck her head past the trees but did nothing else, as if afraid of what might lurk just beyond.

Rick couldn't blame her. He never wanted to venture into the forest again if he could help it. He wasn't even interested in fishing anymore. "We were separated," he said.

Tika, Brent, and Curtis came over. "Separated?" Joanne said.

"We were chased by a pig." It sounded ridiculous when he heard it said out loud.

"In the dark? And you're okay?" Tika stared at him as if searching for obvious injuries.

"It went after Danny," Rick said. He watched Tika's expression. Her eyes dropped away, and she looked at the wet, muddy ground. "He's going to show up. He had a head start."

Joanne nodded.

Curtis didn't have a camera with him. Rick couldn't blame him. He was tired of thinking about the television show. They need to extract out of Papua and head home. He'd had enough. "You okay, buddy?"

"I'm good, dude." Curtis ran his palms down his shirt. "They found the kids."

"They did?" Rick said.

Tika nodded. "They're safe. They were never in danger. They'd wandered off despite having been told not to. Kids, you know."

"I'm thankful they're okay," Rick said. He bit his tongue. The amount of danger those kids caused was considerable. Danny was still out there, missing. Maybe injured. Possibly dead. Rick turned to Halperin, "We need to find Danny, and go home."

"All done fishing?"

Rick spun around. Lance Crowley wore a big grin. He liked to show off straight, white teeth.

Rick walked around Joanne and Curtis, and went toward Lance. "How did you come to be here, huh? How did you find out about this? Any of this? I don't think the guy who sent a letter to our network sent one to yours. In fact, his letter was pretty explicit in explaining to us how he felt about you!"

"Let's just say I have an. . .in, and leave it at that."

"An in? Like a spy?" Rick said.

"Leave it alone, Rick." Lance addressed everyone as if on stage or speaking in front of his camera, though none was around. "If you and your team are done, packing it in and heading home, then have a safe trip. I mean that, sincerely. My team and I--we have a creature to catch. It's in that river and we are not planning to stop fishing until we find it."

When Lance turned around and started to walk away, Rick lunged.

Curtis caught him by the arm and pulled him back. "Let it go," he said. "He's a dweeb, ya know?"

Rick shrugged out of the restraint. "We need to find Danny, Halperin. He's been out there all night. We need to find him, and we need to leave."

Rick wasn't sure if Halperin agreed with him or not. The shirt and tie guy was keeping his mouth shut and just kept nodding. It pacified Rick. "I need water."

***

Rick Stone Journal Entry:

I have not seen Tika in over an hour. I need to find out what is going on. My team assembled and assisted in the search for the children. I wanted to know if the Wairoku people were going to step up to the plate and help find Danny. It has been at least eight hours since I have seen him. I did not want to waste daylight sitting around waiting to see who was going to help. The forest was just as dangerous, regardless of time. I just knew I'd feel better looking while the sun was out.

Curtis was running toward him. "Rick! Rick!"

Rick put his pen inside the journal, closed it, and set it next down on the hut's porch. He stood up as Curtis reached him. "What is it?"

"The chief agreed. They're going to help us find Danny."

It was terrific news. "When are we going out to look?"

"They're getting ready. We're going right now."

"Not we. I want you to stay here. Watch over our stuff. I don't trust Lance or his groupies," Rick said. It was true. He did not trust Lance at all, but he wasn't worried about their things. Let Lance steal everything they brought, even footage of the trip. He just did not want to put Curtis in any more danger than he had to.

"I am not staying--"

"Rick!" Joanne ran up to the hut. "They found him!"

"Found him? Found who? Danny?"

"Biak and Prai went looking for him as soon as you came out of the forest. They're back. They have Danny."

"He's okay?"

"Twisted ankle. I don't think it's broken, though. Maybe too swollen to know for sure."

The three of them headed for the center of the village, Joanne in the lead.

Tika knelt next to Danny. He was sprawled out on a makeshift stretcher. Danny waved.

Rick thought he might cry. "I knew we'd find you."

"No, you didn't. You thought I was dead," Danny said.

"Yeah. Yes, I did. You're right." Rick laughed. The tension that had been warping his gut unraveled, and he felt like he could breathe more normally despite the thick humidity.

"I *know* I'm right. I thought I was a goner myself."

Rick squatted down on the other side of Danny. "How'd this happen?"

"Pig chased me, not very far. I toppled down some hill, and kept falling and falling. I landed next to the river. It stopped at the top of the embankment, thank God. I swear I could hear it breathing up there. Angry breathing, and just when I was sure it was going to come down after me, I must have passed out. When I opened my eyes, Biak and Prai had me on this thing and were dragging me through the trees. Mosquitos had a field day with my blood, let me tell you. You see fat bugs built like me, then you know who they feasted on last night!" When Danny laughed, it made the direness of the situation seem light and humorous.

"Can I get you anything?" Rick said.

"I'd kill for a beer, burger, and fries. Think that's asking for too much?"

Rick held his thumb and finger close together. "A wee bit."

"Something to drink sounds good. Some of that alcohol fruity stuff from the other night would hit the spot," Danny said.

"I bet we can get you some," Rick said, and looked at Tika for help.

"I'll handle it," she said.

They were far from free and clear. Rick said, "We'll have to get him to a doctor. He's going to need to have that leg bone set."

She nodded. "We can have Prai take him back toward town."

"We're all going back," Rick said.

"We can't do that." Halperin stood over Rick.

Rick stood up. "I told you earlier. We needed to find Danny, and then we were all going home. We have Danny. Thank God, he's safe. Now we're going back. All of us. This is over. You want to fire me, cancel the show, fine, but I'm done. You hear me? Done."

Curtis followed after Rick as he stormed off.

"Rick, Rick?"

Only once he reached the hut did Rick stop. "What?"

"I'm with you. We should get out of here. This place is dangerous to people like us. We don't belong. We weren't raised here. Everything around us is a potential hazard. I get it. I do."

"Thank you."

"But . . ." Curtis said.

Rick sighed. "*But* what?"

"We're here. We have close to enough footage to give the network what they need to make some serious shows. Think about everything we've filmed already. If we spend just another day on the water fishing--get some solid casting done, whether we catch that thing in the river or not, we're golden, man. Dude, golden. I got your back. You say we go, I'm with you. But, man, I need this job, and if not this job, then I need some more footage to sharpen the edges of my resume. You understand what I'm saying? Can you see what I'm asking you? If we go back now, who knows how the network will handle this. We signed some lengthy contracts. I didn't read much past the first page, you know?"

Rick pursed his lips. He wanted to fire back a retort that would make his point clear, but couldn't. Everything Curtis said made sense. Luckily, Danny was alright. "One more night. It's all I'm doing. We only come off that river to eat and sleep."

Curtis smiled. "That's what I'm talking about."

"First, we make sure Danny is good with this. His foot might not be broken but if he wants to head back, we're going back. Deal?"

"Fair enough."

CHAPTER 20

Rick stood along the riverbank. He had some fruit and nibbled at it, not really hungry. Just on the other side of the tethered pirogue were two birds. Each was nearly as tall as he was. They looked like colorful emus, except their heads had a solid brown ridge like the back spine of a dinosaur.

"They are Cassowary. The bright one, the taller one there, is the female." Tika stood next to him. He was not sure when she had arrived. Her voice should have startled him out of his thoughts. It soothed him instead.

"They are beautiful."

"And endangered. For the most part."

"Those heads look pretty dangerous," Rick said.

"Like a battering ram." Tika punched a fist into her palm, but smiled. "Although it's not their skull I'd watch out for. They have a single talon that is like a dagger. If they feel threatened, they can slash out with it. Disembowel you right where you stand."

"A pleasant thought." Rick tried to laugh. He kept his eyes on the birds. He wasn't afraid. The canoes separated them, and he had no intention of showing any aggression toward either of the Cassowary. He worried more about revealing feelings if Tika saw into his eyes. Rick held up a piece of his fruit. "May I?"

Tika shrugged.

Rick tossed a section of fruit toward the Cassowary. They looked up at him. They stood still, perhaps hoping they would not be seen.

Rick tossed over a second piece.

The Cassowary approached the fruit cautiously. They ate it. They looked over at Rick. He threw over what he had left. Tika and he watched the birds eat in silence. When finished with the tiny meal the Cassowary moved about by the water before jogging back into the thicket of the rain forest. Rick would have to remember to tell his son about some of the amazing things he'd seen on this trip. So much of it so surreal.

"Are you alright?" Tika placed a hand on his shoulder. It was as if she did not need to see into his eyes to get a view of his soul. For being that easy to read, Rick was almost embarrassed.

"I just want to catch this fish and go home." It was true, but not what he had been thinking.

"Do you have a family waiting?"

"A wife and a son. Jared. He's just a baby," he said.

"That's wonderful."

He shrugged, silently amazed at Tika's perception. She might have said 'that's wonderful,' but he heard the tone of her voice. It was as if she already knew his family life fell short of anything resembling wonderful.

"You don't think so?"

"My son is the best part of my life."

Tika smiled.

"There's nothing I wouldn't do for him."

"A proud father. I can hear it in your voice," Tika said. "And your wife must be very proud of you. Star of your own show."

Rick hoped he smiled. The muscles in his mouth felt strained. "You would think."

"What? She is not proud of you? I don't believe that."

"Well," Rick shrugged and turned away from the water.

***

"If you are not one-hundred percent sure, then we are going back," Rick said.

Danny wore a broad grin. The alcohol provided by the tribe had him under the influence. "Seriously, Rick, we're good. Go. Go fishing. I'm fine. I got this giant leaf umbrella pretending to keep me dry, the naked native ladies to watch as they bustle all over the place, bouncing here and bouncing there, and. . .and the best part, I seem to have an endless supply of Poison Frog."

"Poison *what*?"

"Frog. *This*." He held up his glass. "Whatever this is. They don't really have a name for it. I mean, they might. They called it something, but I have no clue what they said. I decided to name it. Think they have poison frogs here?"

"I really am not sure."

Danny waved a hand through the air. "No matter. It's what I'm calling it. Would you care to partake?"

"Was that an Australian accent?"

"Australian or Scottish." Danny gurgled out what could have been a coughing laugh. "Eh, mate."

"We're not in Australia."

"Close though. Closer than we are to Scotland."

"You've got a point."

"But you know what I struggle most with? The guys here. I'm hung like a thumb. I could probably shove my penis back into myself, but I can't figure out the 'why' about it?"

"You circumcised?"

"I am."

"Show them how you had the tip of yours chopped off, see if they are any less confused by your actions."

Danny looked befuddled. "That, Rick, that was my parents. They did this to me. I shoulda been a lot bigger. A lot bigger. Damn doctor had a hacking obsession, let me tell you. Look, sit down. Why don't I pour you some Poison Frog?"

"Never when I fish, and I'm about to go out now," Rick said.

"You going to catch that monster swimming in their river?"

"It's the plan."

"I'll drink to that," Danny said, and chugged.

"You're all right then?"

Danny pursed his lips tight. Rick knew his friend was doing his best to look serious, professional. "I will be fine."

"We're leaving tomorrow though, regardless."

"And I am fine with that, too."

Rick stood up.

"If you see my waitress, please tell her I am ready to look at a menu now." Danny lost it. He laughed hard and slapped his hand onto his thigh. "I'm ready to look at my menu now!"

CHAPTER 21

The rain just kept falling. The weather was relentless. The river ran swift, the water levels high. Rick could not imagine living under these conditions. Curtis had been correct pointing out they didn't belong on this island, in the middle of the vast rain forest.

"With Danny out of commission, I'm going to need you to man his camera, Joanne. You can ride on the same boat with me. You basically point and shoot. Film everything. Editing can do their job when we get back. You okay with that?" Rick knelt by his gear, shuffled through his tackle box to make sure everything was packed properly.

"I can do that."

"It's a real easy camera to use," Curtis said. For a few moments, Rick watched as Curtis gave Joanne a quick lesson. "It's not like we're far from each other. If you have a question, I'm just a boat over."

Halperin looked pale; his skin pasty. The sweat on his face made him look more like a zombie than a human. It beaded, stuck on his skin, as opposed to the rainwater that ran down his cheeks. "Lance and his crew are already out there. He's not a nice guy. It's like cutthroat to him. So let's get these people moving. I want us to get out there and catch this fish before he does. Am I making myself clear?"

"Oh, crystal, Brent. Crystal."

Halperin clapped his hands. "We ready?"

Rick bit down on his upper lip. It was the only physical thing he could think to do that stopped him from starting an argument with one of his bosses. "Give us a few minutes. Why don't you go sit on your pirogue and wait while we finish double checking and loading gear."

Halperin was lazy and had done little to lift a finger the entire time. Rick didn't think his boss expected the conditions to be as raw as they were. All those packed silk ties serving no purpose at all had to depress someone who considered himself so important.

Once everything was on each of the boats, Prai and Biak took them back out onto the river. Rick's assessment was correct. The water moved far faster than before. The whine of small outboard motors straining against the current was proof enough.

Rick spoke to his unseen audience. The lights from the cameras nearly blinded him amidst the dark gloom of cloud coverage. "There are so many fish native to these waters. Aside from the Bull Shark, I can't think of a fish with enough teeth or strength to do the damage I observed on the Wairoku man. We still have some special bait that we're going to use. Hopefully the meat and blood associated with it will attract the monster swimming in this river."

Rick went to work affixing the slabs of pig organ onto his hooks. "Because I am not sure what kind of fish we're dealing with, I am going to cast a few lines. One will go as close to the banks as possible. The other, I am just going to drop off the side. As you can see, the rains are relentless. Although I have not been here long, even I notice the water levels appear higher than they were a day ago, and the water is moving fast. The current is so swift, I feel as if it would challenge even some of the best swimmers in the world."

At least an hour passed. Rick did plenty of catching and releasing. The river was full of hungry fish, just not creatures. He was close to giving up, calling it a night, and ending the trip.

Then his line went taut. There was more than a tug. Something bit into the bait. Rick didn't want to react prematurely. If he wasn't cautious, he'd yank on his fishing pole too soon. That would startle the fish. It would swim away.

He waited.

Waited.

Yanking on the rod, he knew the hook pierced the fish. "Fish on!" He cranked the reel. The fish fought back.

Rick felt the power on the opposite end. It opposed his every move. "It's swimming. I'm giving it some line. Letting it go."

The sound of the spool spinning was musical. The idea of notes filled his vision as he tugged on the line.

"This is big. Whatever is on that hook, it's big. It's not going to give up easily. This might just prove to be a battle. As long as my line doesn't snap, I'm going to win. Unfortunately, the fish doesn't realize that yet," Rick said. He knew Curtis was filming, and hoped that Joanne was as well. This was what the trip was about. Right here. Now.

"What scares me is that I have no idea what the riverbed is like. If it is rocky and this fish swims along the bottom, the line will get worn and could be cut, freeing the fish. I don't want to let that happen. I'm letting him fight right now. It will tire him out. He's in a panic. He knows something's not right. There's a hook in his mouth and some invisible force is working against him.

"I am that invisible force."

Thirty minutes passed. Rick kept reeling the fish in, and then gave him some line to swim away before reeling it in once again. It was a game. Might be the first time for the fish. It was the millionth for Rick.

"Deep sea fishing for swordfish once, I spent two and a half hours struggling against a fish on my line. I was harnessed in, sitting in a chair, my feet rested on a platform. Other fishermen on the boat brought me water and wiped sweat from my brow. It is ideal fishing conditions. Out here, I'm on a long thin canoe. Standing is going to be dangerous. If this fish fights much more, there is a serious chance he could pull me right over the side. If the pirogue capsizes, that would be dangerous for not just me, but my crew as well."

The fight raged on. Rick felt it in his hands, arms and shoulders. The muscles were tight. There was no way to shake it off. He needed to keep a tight grip on the rod. If he loosened it for even a fraction of a second, he could have the pole pulled from his hands and all this time spent on the river would be for nothing. . .and make for lousy television.

There was a loud splash in the water. It was several feet from the boat.

"I see it!" Rick nodded with his head. "Can we get a light over there?"

Curtis swiveled his camera and aimed it at the water. "Joanne, don't take the camera off Rick. There's more than one, Rick. I got movement on the surface of the water. All over the place!"

"I don't know if my cameraman caught that, but I saw the fish. It was big. Definitely not a Bull Shark, I cannot say for sure, but I may know what it is, and if I'm right, it is not common in these waters. It could explain the aggressive behavior, finding itself in new surroundings. Perhaps getting accustomed to the native food," Rick said.

Something jumped in the water.

"Got it, I got it!" Curtis said. "Thing came right out of the water. Had a huge set of teeth! Thing had to be, I don't know five and a half, maybe six feet long. Huge!"

"Six feet long!" Rick smiled. "That makes me extra apprehensive. The line is stretched tight. It has already undergone plenty of stress. I do not want this to snap. I can't imagine letting the river creature responsible for an untold amount of Wairoku disappearances and deaths get away!"

The line went limp.

Rick stood still. He slowly reeled in more line. And a little more. And some more.

"It's under the boat," he said, whispering. He sat down. "If he hits us and I'm standing, I'll be going overboard. I bet it would like nothing more than to get a taste of me, I'm sure."

Rick wanted to wait the fish out.

He didn't want to agitate it. "You think you got a good look at the fish on film?"

"Absolutely," Curtis said. "If I had any artistic skill, I could draw it for you."

Rick felt good. They had it. This fish, the one on his line, had to be the culprit responsible. It made the most sense. It was far, far away from home. How it got into these waters was another story. People were always introducing fish into foreign bodies of water. The outcome was rarely good, the ecology suffered.

The fish hit the bottom of Rick's pirogue. He dropped the pole. He grabbed onto the sides of the boat. He dropped his feet onto the rod's handle. This thing was not going to get away that easily.

Curtis said, "You guys okay? I got it. Caught it. Looked like you guys were going to tip."

Rick didn't care that Curtis was talking so much. The audio was likely to suck anyway. They could do voice-overs at the network studio. This was going to be an amazing series. The viewing audience was likely to double. Triple, even.

With his fishing rod back in hand, Rick stayed seated. He was worried about standing. It might make for good TV if he fell into the river, but Rick didn't consider his death as an ideal circumstance to boost ratings.

The motor on the boat was off. The fish had dragged them further up the river, against the current. The beast was quite strong. "It is always hard to gauge the weight of a fish when you're fighting the line. They always feel like whales. This one, it's a whale. Not literally," Rick laughed. "But if I had to guess, I'd put it at one-fifty, maybe as much as one hundred and seventy-five pounds. It weighs as much as I do. It's all muscle. Probably no fat at all on its body. In a fair fight, I am not sure who I'd place my money on."

The line pulled tight. Rick let it spin. It shred yard after yard in seconds. "It's on the run!"

He needed to control the fight, show the fish he was the one in charge. He fought back, pulling on the rod, when the unthinkable happened.

The line broke.

Snapped.

Rick stood up, stared at the ripple in the river.

He wanted to see the fish again, one last time.

Even if he cast a new line, fresh bait, that thing wasn't coming back. It wouldn't bite again, not tonight. Not unless there was more than one. Curtis swore there could be more than one.

Halperin screamed. Their boat rocked. Halperin rolled off the side. He splashed into the water, went below the surface for just a moment. His head came up. He shook it like a wet dog. His hands clasped onto the side of the pirogue. "Get me out of this river," Halperin said. He could not hide the fear in his voice.

Rick had to bite at the insides of his cheeks. Otherwise, he would laugh. Nothing like seeing a boss fall into a river. "Get him out, guys. Pull him out of there."

Halperin's mouth opened wide. No sound escaped his lips for a long moment. "It's got me! It's biting me."

Curtis set down his camera. The fun over. He reached over the side of the boat. He latched his hands onto the back of Halperin's pants and yanked, pulling his boss back into the boat.

The skin on Halperin's leg was scraped deep and bleeding. It looked like fingernails raked across a wall with drying paint. "It's not that bad."

"You sure?" Rick said.

Curtis unzipped a First Aid kit. "He's ripped up a bit."

"Am I going to lose the leg," Halperin said. He huffed and puffed. Rick was certain he'd hyperventilate.

"Settle down, Halperin. Breathe in, hold it. Breathe out. Okay? Take it easy. Curtis is going to bandage you," Rick said.

"I'm going to lose my leg, huh?"

"Hey, stop it. You're scratched."

"It bit me. It didn't scratch me."

"He's right," Curtis said. There was little light to work with. Joanne filmed. She shined the light onto Halperin's leg. "The skin is flayed, but the teeth went in deep."

"Can you stop the bleeding?" Rick said.

"I'm going to try. Hang tight, boss. I'm going to put some ointment on there. Kills germs. No idea what kind of bacteria thrives out here. Foreign, regardless. We don't want you getting some bizarre infection." Curtis winked at Rick. What had been said was true, but it was said purely to terrorize the boss.

Joanne said, "So we got the fish on film and an attack. Wow."

Rick thought. *Yeah. Hot damn.*

***

"Those Crowley's boats?"

Rick looked over to where Brent Halperin pointed. The pirogues were on the left bank, out of the water, and up on the land. "Looks like it."

Halperin never said he wanted to go back to the village. Once the bleeding stopped and the bandages were on good and tight, he'd suggested more fishing. Rick hated to admit he was impressed.

Biak and Prai talked to each other. Rick followed the volley and in between, eyed Tika. He hoped she planned to translate. Whatever the guides discussed, they seemed animated about the topic.

"Tika?"

She didn't respond. Instead, she appeared equally engrossed in the conversation. When Biak and Prai stopped talking, the three of them looked at Rick.

Rick didn't need a sixth sense to know something had just changed. "What? What's going on?"

"You need to get your hooks back into the boat. We need to get back to the Wairoku village," Tika said. Rick thought she was trying to seem calm. He could tell by the mechanical way she was breathing. In and out. In and out. Very calculated. Not too quick. Not too shallow. The truth was in her eyes and how wide open they were.

"I really just need to catch a few hours of footage of me fishing, and then we're done. Packing it in and leaving."

Joanne lowered her camera.

A director should know better. It might be her first time manning a camera, but the rules hadn't changed. Rick gritted his teeth. "Keep it rolling, Joanne. We document everything."

"We need to get back to the village. This is non-negotiable, I'm afraid," Tika said.

Rick wasn't about to cave that easy. He wanted to get off this island and back home more than anyone. The idea of wrapping up without enough film made the entire trip for nothing. He'd be out of a job. They all would. Harry Krantz would have no choice but to issue pink slips. Only thing that would make it worse, like salt rubbed into a raw wound, would be if a show aired on *Casting with Lance Crowley* in their stead. "I know this doesn't seem important to you, us fishing for a television show, but we need to figure out what is in this river. We need to get it on camera. Our livelihoods depend on it."

"Your lives depend on getting back to the village," Tika said.

"That's a little melodramatic, don't you think?" Rick said. He looked to Halperin for help. The man was a mere mannequin. If it wasn't about fashion, he was useless. He filed away all the help Halperin did not deliver. If anything, Krantz would hear about the ineffectiveness of the network's right-hand-man. "The other team here, Lance and his people, they're out there doing something. Getting film of--"

"They're dead."

Tika's words stopped Rick cold. He stared at her, waiting for more, suddenly aware of the thundering sound of the river and the occasional caw of birds within the rainforest. "I'm sorry, what?"

"Your friend Lance--"

"He's no friend of ours," Curtis said, and then snickered.

Tika shot Curtis a look, her eyes narrowed, her upper lip curled. "Your friend and his team, they're dead."

"Wait. Wait," Rick said. He stood in the boat. Tika reached for his arm. Rick pulled away. The boat wobbled. Rick regained his balance but did not sit. "Who's dead? Lance? Tyson? Jerry? Albert? What do you mean they're dead?"

Tika never looked away. She locked eyes with Rick. "See the pirogues? They are on the left bank, upside down."

Rick shrugged, looking. The way it rained, if he pulled the boats out of the water, tipping them made sense. "I see that," Rick said.

Prai started to talk, softly, but fast. Prai had brought his boat right up alongside Biak's. He held his hand on the side, keeping them close together.

Tika held up a hand. She responded to Prai, nodding. "The Yakti Tribe always lifts their pirogues out of the water and lays them upside down."

Rick sat down. His head spun. None of what Tika said made sense. "Tika, please. I am not following you."

She looked at him, head tilted slightly to the side.

Rick rolled his hands. "I don't follow you. I don't. . .understand what you are trying to tell me."

Her eyes widened, as if she now understood the expression. "If the Yakti took your friends' pirogues," Tika looked at Curtis to silence him before he had a chance to voice another outburst without missing a beat, "out of the water, then it is safe to assume your friends are with the Yakti tribe."

"Okay, and. . ."

"And? That is all."

"You told me Lance and his team is dead."

"I suspect they are. We need to get back and talk to Amu as quickly as possible."

Rick looked from Joanne to Curtis and stopped on Halperin. "I am guessing the Yakti are not friendly. That's what you are trying to tell us. Lance and his team, they didn't just voluntarily go with this tribe. They were taken. Abducted."

Tika merely provided confirmation with a slight nod.

"And you think they are going to kill them, all of them?" Rick said.

"I think it might be safe to assume that they're already dead."

Safe to assume? Rick placed an arm across his stomach. He wanted to go home. He'd look for another job. He would work in a factory or a fast food restaurant. Wherever. He would do whatever needed to get done if Krantz served him with his walking papers. Staying on this island any longer just did not make sense. "Okay, Tika, get us back. Take us back to your village."

Tika was silent.

Prai and Biak raised their arms into the air. Halperin's face lost all color.

"Rick," Joanne said. It came in a whisper. Her camera slid from her hands into the bottom of the pirogue.

Rick didn't want to turn around.

When he did, he saw what Curtis intently filmed.

The Yakti had dark colored skin, looked identical to the Wairoku, except that they covered their bodies in painted white designs; bold lines that rolled into patterned circles or were speckled with dots along straight lines that ended abruptly. It reminded Rick of Native American war paint, except it was all one color. The white popped on the dark bodies.

Two things bothered Rick more than the display of war paint, and that was the sheer number of the Yakti and the drawn bows with barbed arrows aimed directly at them.

"What do we do?" Rick said.

Tika said, "What Lance did, I'm guessing. We go ashore."

CHAPTER 22

Rick had the knife on his hip. He was confident the others on his team had one strapped to their sides as well. Five knives would accomplish absolutely nothing. It wasn't that Rick had never stabbed or cut another person before, the problem was that he had never so much as even hit another man. He didn't know how to fight. In school, he got along with anyone. There had been some pushing matches, but they never came down to exchanging blows. It had been close a time or two, but then someone always diffused the situation prior to any slugging getting started.

In a river, under a downpour, Rick's mouth was dry. He nearly gagged trying to swallow as Prai and Biak motored the pirogues toward shore.

"How do we get out of this?" Joanne said. Her lips quivered. She held onto the bench she sat on with both hands. The whites of her knuckles almost glowed in the gloom. "Rick?"

"Shh," he said. There was no answer. He knew Tika was as equally unnerved. There had been warnings she'd dropped since the get-go. The area tribes were not necessarily friendly. "We'll get out of this. We will."

Rick did not look at Tika. After lying to Joanne, he didn't need to see accusations in her eyes.

The front of their pirogue ran up onto dirt and grass. The water level kept rising. The Yakti were silent. They stood like statues, armed and looking dangerous.

"What do we do?" Halperin said, his pirogue next to Rick's.

One of the Yakti men spoke. His voice was shrill, high-pitched. He barked orders. He motioned everyone forward with a swing of his bow. The string was drawn. The arrow, if released, looked as if it would slice through the bridge of Rick's nose.

"They want us to get off the boats," Tika said.

The Yakti leader shouted at her. Yelling, he grabbed her wrist and twisted it, forcing her off the boat and down to her knees.

She spoke to him in their native tongue. It seemed to catch the Yakti off guard. They looked from one to the other.

"I told them I am Wairoku. They find it hard to believe because I am dressed more like all you," she said, slowly getting back up onto her feet. She kept her hands raised in the air, her eyes on the Yakti.

The Yakti focused on Biak and Prai. They got off the boat, hands up.

Rick felt helpless. "What are they saying?"

Tika shot him a look. "Get off the boat. Now."

Rick and the others climbed off the pirogues.

A Yakti walked up to Rick and kicked him in the groin. Rick doubled over. His hands cupped his crotch. Dropping to his knees, he coughed and gagged. Another blow was delivered to his side. Something cracked. He rolled over onto the opposite side, curled into a tight fetal position. Before he could raise his arms to block his head, a third kick crashed into his head. A brilliant display exploded behind closed eyes.

"No one move! No one!"

Rick forced his eyes open. From his position on the wet earth, he cringed. Curtis had drawn a gun. It was Danny's. He looked panicked, pivoting left and right. "Put it away," Rick said.

Curtis ignored him. Both hands clasped on the handle, his finger on the trigger. "Here's what's going to happen. We're going to get back on the boats and leave. No harm no foul! Tell them, Tika."

She said, "Curtis--"

"Tell them!"

The arrow protruded from the center of his chest. His arms dropped to his side. The gun fired a shot into mud. Curtis' eyes went wide, as he looked at Rick. His fingertips brushed across the arrow fletching. The feathers parted and sprang back. He fell, fast, the ground rushed up to meet his face. The sound of an arrow snapping in two was all that Rick heard before his eyes closed and a welcomed darkness consumed him.

***

Rick opened his eyes. The first thing he saw was a large fire. It roared, defying the heavy rainfall. He closed his eyes and gently shook his head. It felt like his brain had become detached from the stem and sloshed around inside his skull. Spots flitted across the back of his eyes. He stomach lurched. He could not recall the last time he'd eaten. He knew he might vomit, regardless.

It came back to him. All of it. Like a wave washing over him. It was cold and slimy and stuck to his skin. He almost screamed -- his mouth opened . . .

"Shh."

Tika was tied to a tall tree stump next to him. Only then did he even realize his arms were behind him, wrists and ankles bound. He tried to steady his vision. He looked around the fire. Tied to trees he saw Halperin, Prai, Biak and Joanne. Her clothing had been ripped off her body. Her head hung low. He had no idea if she was alive. The others were looking around as well. They looked as scared as he felt.

The spit over the fire held a roasted body.

"TIka," he said, he tried to whisper. He tried to hold his emotions in check. "Please tell me that's not Curtis?"

"Please, be quiet. Don't let them hear you talking."

Tika pursed her lips tight. She shook her head. Rick got the message. He held back the scream that threatened to erupt and instead tried to take in their surroundings to assess the situation. There was no way out of this *that* much he knew. They were as good as dead. He didn't want to die. Not here, not like this.

He wanted to see his son again. Needed to hold him one last time. It was a desperate need. It filled him. He didn't hide the tears.

"Stop it," Tika said. "We need to stay calm."

Her whispers barely made it to his ears, the sound of the fire, the rainfall. . .the chanting.

They were around the fire. The Yakti. They wore cloth around their waists, like Tarzan. The women were topless, dancing, breasts bouncing. All of them were covered in the white war paint.

Curtis was dead. Being cooked like a pig over a fire.

They were going to eat him. Savor his flesh.

Rick shook his head. He needed to rid his mind of these thoughts. The nightmare they presented was too much for him to take in. There had to be a way out of this. A way to escape.

A way to get home.

Fooling himself into believing there was an out, a possible way out, didn't work. Couldn't work. Looking around again he could only imagine what flashed through the minds of his friends. Similar thoughts, no doubt. Worse thoughts, probably.

"Can't you talk to them?" Rick chanced talking. No one seemed to be watching him. He wiggled his arms some. His wrists were tightly secured. There was not going to be a way to shake free. "Say something."

"I tried. I've been trying. They've told me to shut up."

Darkness swam in his peripheral. They were perched on the edge, the fire pit the center. The natives kept dancing around the fire. They chanted. There was no drum. Rick thought a drum was needed. In all the movies he'd seen, the cannibalistic natives had drums. They always used drums.

"Will Chief Amu come for us?"

"Please, Rick. Stop talking!" Although a whisper, spoken through clenched teeth, Rick felt the demanding essence of the words spat at him. "My hands are almost free."

Rick stared at Tika. "Free?"

"Shhh."

He saw it then. Her shoulder twitched forward, back, side to side. She was working the rope, or vines, or against whatever material was used to bind them. No wonder she wanted him to shut up. She didn't want him attracting attention.

His mind was a whirlwind. Never in a million years did he imagine he'd be in this type of predicament. His heart hammered away behind his ribcage. He knew he was sweating. He felt the salt of it sting his eyeballs, slide into his mouth, and wet his otherwise dry tongue.

There was no telling how much time they had left, or how long it would take Tika to get free. Time moved in slow motion anyway. It all seemed surreal. Everything played out in front of him as if strobe lights flashed all around him. Bright light. Darkness. Light. Dark. Light. Dark. Lightdark lightdarklightdark.

He still wanted to scream. His lungs demanded it.

His senses worked overtime. Pain burned his wrists and ankles from the bindings. The fire a few feet away crackled like gunshots and sent heat toward him in violent waves. He tasted the salt in his sweat as it dripped into his mouth, and the odor of his own body was rank and raw.

The pungent odor of Curtis on a spit over an open flame.

There was no escaping the smoke from his cooking flesh. It wafted right at him, assaulting his nostrils. He'd never forget the smell. Never.

"I have a hand out," Tika said.

It was the best thing he'd heard in a long time. He wasn't sure what would happen next. Even if she freed her other hand and feet, then what? Would she untie him, or run disappearing into the forest?

The Yakti would notice, right away. If she wasn't secured to that tree, they'd go after her. Wouldn't they? He could just imagine them letting out a rally cry and chasing after her. They would never let her escape so easily.

It wouldn't be easy.

Getting her hand free at all was amazing.

Rick flexed his wrists, twisted his hands. They might not survive this, but they were good as dead if he did nothing and just stood there feeling sorry for himself.

There was no time for self-pity.

Not now.

Not anymore.

"My hands are free," she said.

And the chanting around the fire fell silent.

CHAPTER 23

"Why did the singing stop?" Rick said.

"Shh," Tika said. Although her wrists were free, she kept her arms behind her, hugging the tree at an awkward angle.

Rick snapped his mouth shut. He continued to flex his wrists and turn his arms in as subtle a way as possible. He wanted to get loose of the ties that bound him without any of the Yakti noticing.

He moved as quietly as possible. It seemed like every rub against the bark sounded like a shout amidst the sudden silence. Then the chant started again. A lone female voice. A solo, perhaps. The tempo increased, getting faster and faster, with a harshness to each word uttered. Rick had no clue what was being said. The woman's words commanded a uniform response now and then from those around the fire. In the oddest of ways, Rick could not help but think of Rick James. Thankfully, the chanting grew intense. The natives had not stopped because Tika had wiggled free. It had been merely a pause in the song they sang. The sigh of relief Rick exhaled deflated him so much that he thought he felt some give in the ropes. He'd been that tense.

Out of the corner of his eye, he saw Tika slide along the trunk and use her hands to unfasten the binds around her ankles. She never looked away from the fire in front of her. If the Yakti turned in their direction, she would have no time to stand back up and pretend she was secured. The jig would be up. Her fingers worked fast.

This encouraged Rick. He pulled his arms and shook his body as much as possible. The slight give he'd felt had accomplished only a little. A little was better than nothing. He could not tell if the others were doing the same, fighting against their restraints. The smoke rising off the body and the dancing of the colorful flames made it hard to see across the pit. He hoped they were. He wanted all of them to escape.

"Stay calm," Tika said with her lips by his ear.

"Forget about me. Run. Get back to your village. Bring help."

He felt her fingers on his wrists. Knew she was trying to work loose the knots. As much as he meant what he said, he truly did not want her to leave him stranded if she could free him instead. He wanted the chance to run through the forest and find freedom on the opposite bank.

The chanting stopped.

Rick looked up and gasped. "They know you're gone."

Her hands let go of his wrists, and it was immediately an awful and isolated sensation. He heard fallen branches snap. She was running. Hopefully, fast. She needed to be fast because the Yakti did not hesitate. An army of tribesmen took off after her. They were armed with bows, arrows, blow darts, and crudely crafted hatchets.

Rick heard Halperin crying out. "Don't leave me here! Please! Please!"

Rick wanted to shout out to his boss telling him to shut the hell up, but couldn't. Didn't. He felt the same way. Stranded. Alone.

They ran past where he was still tied to the tree, a blur of painted men were on his left and on his right.

"Don't leave us here! Tika!" Halperin shouted.

A Yakti appeared in front of Rick. The paintwas precise on his face. He grunted and chomped his teeth near Rick's nose. Rick maintained his composure. He was frightened. He was not going to let it show. They would not get that satisfaction.

Someone behind him pulled the ropes tight against his extremities. He knew his skin had done more than chafe. It was ripped open and blood oozed. Circulation was being cut off. If he stayed like this for any period of time, his hands and feet would die, be like lifeless appendages at the end of immobile limbs.

The man in front of him grunted again. He stepped back and raised a hatchet. He tossed it from hand to hand. It was simple back and forth. For some reason, it looked far more clever and fascinating the way it was done. Rick could not help but follow the hand-sized weapon with his eyes. It mesmerized him.

The tribesman pulled the hatchet back behind his head and swung.

As much as Rick wanted to appear cool, calm and collective, he lost and screamed. His eyes were shut tight. He could not imagine watching a blade sink into his chest.

Only it didn't. He was not hacked open.

Rick's eyelids fluttered.

The Painted Face in front of him smiled. He was messing with Rick and knew it. Psychological torture from cannibals living in a jungle.

Before Rick knew what he was doing, he spat into the man's face. The wadded ball of saliva splashed between the eyes of the Painted Face's nose. It oozed down toward both eyes. It was the wrong move. Rick knew it. "I'm done being messed with. You going to kill me, huh? Cook me? Then do it! Just kill me. Get it over with!"

The tribesman's grin fell away. His eyes narrowed. Rick saw the decay and rot of exposed teeth as the Painted Face let out an animalistic snarl.

The Painted Face pressed the blade--which was merely a sharpened rock--of the hatchet up near Rick's left shoulder. He drew it down and across Rick's chest. The applied pressure and the slow drag made Rick scream as the jagged edges of the rock cut through his skin. Falling rain mixed with spilled blood.

He then cut from the right shoulder across and down to the left. The pain shot through Rick's entire abdomen. "Stop it! Stop it!"

The tribesman licked the blood from the hatchet, his eyes never looking away from Rick's.

Rick watched the man turn and slowly walk back toward the fire. He walked around it and toward Halperin. Rick watched in horror as the Painted Face delivered punishing blows to Brent's face and stomach, punch after punch. The screams that first came from his boss abruptly stopped, even though the beating did not.

**

The dinner plates were made out of wood. Nothing fancy, very rustic.

Curtis' body was removed from the flame and set on a spit off to the side. They cut and stabbed into him with knives and hatchets and dug into him with bare hands. They peeled meat from the bone, and chunked bites out of his thighs with their jagged teeth.

Rick vomited more than once. Dry heaves. Strapped to the tree made it difficult when his stomach muscles tightened, and his back and shoulder blades spasmed with each retch. Thick gooey fluid spurted from his mouth and drooled down his chin. He welcomed the acidic smell of his vomit. It burned his throat and nostrils. It worked as a blanket to mask Curtis' charred flesh.

He saw them walk toward him. Three of them. They carried something behind their back, and when they stood in front of him, held a plate under his face.

Rick looked up and away. This would haunt him forever. He did not want to see his friend carved on a plate.

Painted Face, as he now came to refer to him, fisted Rick's hair and forced his head down. He held it firmly in place. The man was sinewy and strong. Not an ounce of fat on his body. It was all muscle and bone.

Rick kept his eyes closed. He'd be damned if he let them force his eyes open. They were not--

The slap came out of nowhere, and then another, and a third. His face stung. It was all to the right cheek. It sounded like a bell ding-donging inside his skull. If he didn't suffer from a concussion already, these hits would not help.

He opened his eyes, just slightly, and then closed them again.

More slaps. Harder. This time they were to his other cheek. Open palm whacks.

He opened his eyes again. Nothing was in focus. The three faces before him spun around, and blurred and were backlit by the dancing flames from the bon fire.

Rick started to close his eyes again. It wasn't to keep from seeing Curtis' flesh on a plate, it was because he felt confident he was about to pass out. He welcomed the darkness.

Painted Face raised his hand.

Rick opened his eyes.

Painted Face lowered his hand.

They wanted him awake, alert, to see what they had brought over on a wooden plate.

If only that had been the end of it.

Painted Face lifted meat off the plate. He waved it in front of Rick's eyes.

In front of his nose.

"No," Rick said. He hated begging for them to stop. There was no other choice. They might not speak english, but they knew what he said. "No, please. No."

He knew tears crested his eyes.

Painted Face took the top of Rick's head in one hand, and his jaw in the other.

Rick closed his mouth tight.

Painted Face let go, and then punched Rick, hard. Rick spat out a tooth. The three tribesmen laughed. The man on the opposite side punched Rick. It seemed like the only reason was to see if he could knock out a tooth as well. Rick felt his eyes swell, and spat. There was no tooth in the spit, but he hoped he could fool them into thinking there was.

They cheered.

It must have worked. The punches stopped, for now.

This time Painted Face grabbed Rick by the mouth and pulled his jaws open.

Rick couldn't beg. He couldn't speak. He knew if he bit down, bit Painted Face, then the beatings would become relentless.

The alternative. . .

The meat, Curtis, was shoved into his mouth.

Painted Face said something. Primal grunting. He pushed down on Rick's head, and pushed up on his jaw.

Rick was not going to eat Curtis. It wasn't going to happen. He used his tongue and pushed the meat out of his mouth. The taste of it inside his mouth would never go away.

Painted Face slapped more meat against Rick's face. It didn't matter that Rick had his mouth closed. Someone punched him in the stomach. He was affixed to the tree and couldn't double over. The meat was finger fed into his mouth as his lungs demanded air.

His mouth was slammed shut.

His nose was swollen, filled with blood. He had trouble breathing.

Painted Face was not going to be satisfied until Rick ate parts of Curtis.

Rick kept pushing with his tongue, trying to get the meat out of his mouth.

The ties around Rick's hands and ankles were severed.

Painted Face pulled him down, dropped him onto his back on the wet, muddy ground. He kneeled on top of Rick's chest.

Rick turned his head and spat out the meat.

Painted Face balled his hands into a fist. He punched Rick in the face. His nose flattened against his skull as blood sprayed. The crunch echoed inside his ears.

Another tribesman came back with more meat in his hands. He laid it on the wood plate. Painted Face picked up a long cut, and dangled it over Rick's face.

Rick had no idea how he was going to get out of this. There was no compromise. None. He closed his mouth tightly and rolled his lips in, bit down on them.

The punches came again. Rick's head was thrust left and right with each blow. The flitting stars that filled the darkness behind his eyelids were explosive.

When Rick opened his eyes, he was moving. Fast. He was not on his feet. He was on his back. He was being dragged by the ankles through the mud. There were tribesmen all around him, their faces blended, mixed, and rolled with the stars in the night sky, and the raindrops that fell. It seemed like an acid trip. A bad acid trip.

Then the dragging stopped.

Rick didn't try to move. Didn't want to risk any more beatings.

He was tugged, and the earth he'd been dragged along disappeared.

He was over nothing.

And falling.

He fell.

Kept falling.

He screamed! He screamed until all he saw was nothing and darkness filled in all the places where there once was light.

CHAPTER 24

Tika knew the forest. She knew the land. She did not, however, know it from this side of the river. She knew she needed to head south. If she went far enough south, she could cross the river and reach her people. She worried the warriors chasing her would think the same thing. For all she knew they planned to cut her off, running at her from an angle.

She did the opposite.

She ran north-west. She didn't want to get too far away from the river. The thought of getting lost never entered her mind. The further she ran away from the Yakti, the more ground she'd have to cover once she cross the water. It would take longer. She had no idea how long Rick and the others had. Not long.

Growing up Wairoku, she knew better than to run through the forest at night. It was dangerous. Despite attending college in Australia, Tika could not shake fears that had been instilled in her since birth. Irrational or not, spirits lurked behind or up in trees, or worse, buried in shrubs she stepped on.

She tried not to think about it. She tried to focus on the run and her escape. It was far too easy to trip. If she fell, she was as good as done. The Yakti knew how to track; were experts at it. Dangerous.

While the Wairoku used logs in the mud for better footing on the path from the river to the village, the Yakti used the bones of enemies. It served a dual purpose. It provided the desired footing, but also warned nearby and foreign tribes, both hostile and friendly, to stay away. The threat of imminent danger could not be made clearer.

Tika concentrated on her breathing. She didn't want to hyperventilate. She worried she would tire quickly. She was not accustomed to running this fast or this far. There had been a time when she was svelte and limber, muscle and lean. She could climb ropes to the tops of the tallest trees with just her upper body strength.

It had been a long time since she'd done that. Too long.

Once away from the village, it seemed like the only times she returned was for special occasions, or when working as a guide for special tourists.

Over the sound of labored breathing, Tika could not tell for sure how far ahead she was of the Yakti. It did not make sense to stop and listen. Stopping when she still had the ability to run would be nothing less than foolishness. They would be all over her. She knew what happened to women caught by the Yakti. The tribe treated women worse than a pet and enemy women in their possession prayed to *Ginol Silamtena*, their God, for mercy, for death.

She was not going to stop running.

Her legs pumped hard. Northwest.

She knew it was going to be a long way, deep into the forest before she could simply head northeast. She'd need to find a safe place to cross the river. Along her village, the banks were narrow enough to risk swimming. There were parts where the banks were hundreds of yards wide. With how much rain they'd received, the water was high and fast. Currents were strong.

A log.

She could find a log and float on it. Let the current pull her along, and she'd kick and eventually guide it to the opposite bank. That would work. It would have to.

It was time. She had no idea how long she had been running.

She hoped the Yakti were fooled altogether and they had gone in the opposite direction. It was a small, a simple wish, but it could mean the difference between life and death.

Not just hers.

Others depended on her.

She fought the urge to look back. It was tempting. Her mind made her feel like the Yakti were right behind her; like a hand was inches away from snagging her by the shoulder or hair. Her legs only moved so fast. The darkness, the terrain, it worked against her. Every step she took, she risked twisting or breaking an ankle.

She breathed more slowly, quick, but shallow breaths.

She only smelled wet moss. It grew everywhere, on rocks, trees, and fallen limbs.

It was going to be difficult to convince Chief Amu to help the film crews. He did not want them visiting in the first place. It was nothing new. He'd always preached that outsiders were bad, saying they would harm the village. Amu would not go up against the Yakti, would not demand their safe return. There was no way he would. He might even be happy to be done with them.

Explaining to him the importance of saving strangers from some foreign country would not go over well. The chief had no real concept of the world beyond his trees. It was only a few decades ago that the Wairoku became aware of other people besides the villages that surrounded them. Spotting planes in the sky had everyone praying to *Ginol Silamtena* night and day.

It was contact with missionaries when Wairoku first met people with white skin and funny clothing. They preached about a God different from *Ginol Silamtena*. Their visits were not well received at first.

The idea of medicine was introduced.

People did not live long lives in their forest. Few reached grandparent stature. Disease came from all around them. The missionaries tried to explain that with inoculations and medications, many people could grow old and become grandparents. It didn't prevent the Wairoku from praying to their god or their herbalist from performing his duties to care for the people. What the missionaries brought, though, helped. The chief now and the chiefs of the past could not deny that, try as they might.

Tika stopped.

Her mind felt like it was on fire.

She couldn't stop thinking about things that were not important. It was a defense mechanism, her brain's way of taking her mind off the stitch in her side, the fear that pulsed through her veins and arteries with each breath she took. She could not run any longer, not another step further.

She sat and hid behind the tree trunk she was closest too. Pulling her knees in tight, she wrapped her arms around her legs and closed her eyes. She strained to hear anything and everything that moved around her. The forest was alive at night. Sounds came from everywhere, even above.

Tika's imagination overtook her. Ran wild. In her mind's eye she saw large spiders on branches overhead lowering upside down on a silky thread. Snakes slithered toward her feet, using the darkness and ground cover to camouflage an imminent attack. Wild pigs kept quiet as they silently sniffed for her exact whereabouts. Once they had her pinned down, they would crash through the brush and crush her under their massive weight.

She shook her head, an attempt to chase dark thoughts and images from her mind. There was only one sense of salvation, she realized. She opened her eyes. Although she could not see a thing, she looked right and left. She looked up, and then straight ahead.

The sounds of everything around her were not sounds of the Yakti sneaking up.

It was more than possible that her diversion worked, it was likely. The Yakti warriors had run south, along the river, not north, and certainly not northeast, or she would not still be sitting beneath the tree contemplating. . .life. She would be dead by now.

She allowed a slight smile to alter her facial expression. There was hope. The plan could once again be simpler. All she needed to do was keep quiet and head west toward the river. Cross it. Lastly, convince Chief Amu to send Wairoku to rescue what was left of the film crew.

CHAPTER 25

"Rick. Rick?"

Rick felt his body being gently rolled side to side.

"Rick?"

Someone groaned. It might have been him. He opened his eyes. Eyes looked back at him. The head was outlined in a halo of light. It could be an angel. He might be dead.

He couldn't imagine needing to be shaken awake and in such pain if he were in Heaven.

Who'd said he'd go to Heaven.

He turned on his side and dry heaved.

"You okay, Rick?"

Rick placed his forearm over his eyes, shielding them from the light.

The light was the sun.

He could not remember having seen the sun since landing on the island. How many days ago was it now? He wasn't sure. Not many. More than two. Less than a week. Or had it been longer?

The sun had remained hidden the entire time. With it out, it was a good indication the rain stopped.

"How are you feeling? Rick, can you hear me?"

"Lance? Is that you?"

"It's me. They threw you down here last night. It was too dark. I didn't know it was you until this morning. I had no idea what they'd tossed down here with me. I'm sorry," he said.

Rick sat up. They were deep in a hole. The walls were supported by tree bark up to halfway. It probably helped prevent but not completely stop a cave-in. The Yakti did not care if its prisoners died, he'd wager. "What are you sorry for?"

"If I'd of known it was you, I would have tried helping you sooner," he said.

The pit was deep, but not wide. The circumference couldn't be more than twenty or twenty-five feet. "Forget it. Forget about it. Where's your crew? Where is the rest of your team?"

"I don't know. They killed Jerry and Albert. Shot them with these stupid bows. Just bent sticks with string, but they're good. They hit what they aim at. They dropped both of them as we got off the boats. I didn't know what was happening, you know? Our guides told us we had to go ashore, and I was like, that's a bad idea, man. That's a really bad idea. We should just, like, hunker down in the boats, and gun the engine. Make it back to our village, but they argued with me, said we'd be dead from poisonous darts in seconds. I don't see the benefit here. Dying from a poisonous dart, you know, that might have been the better way to go. Quick and over. Done. Now look at us. Look where we are. And I have no clue where Tyson is. He was with me. He had his camera with him, but they split us up. They took him one way, and they dropped me down here," Lance said.

There had to be parts of the story that Lance either forgot or left out on purpose. He'd been roughed up some. His left eye was black and blue, nearly swollen shut. His lips were fat and split. His shirt had been shredded. Rick looked for signs of a hatchet carving initials into Lance's chest, but didn't see any lacerations. Had the natives not cut him? Had they not eaten Lance's crew in front of Lance?

"You look a mess, man," Lance said.

"I was just thinking the same thing about you." Rick smiled and then laughed.

Lance laughed, sat with his back to the makeshift wall, his knees drawn to his chest. He chewed on loose skin around his thumb. "We've got to get out of here. If we just sit here, we're going to die."

"It's got to be like a pantry or refrigerator," Rick said. "You know, without the coolant."

"What? Down here. Why do you say that?"

"Never mind." Rick didn't want to scare Lance, nor did he wish to talk about it. "You're right though. We need to escape."

"You think they're asleep?"

"Who?"

"The natives, who do you think?"

"Why do you think that," Rick said, "that they're asleep?"

"Well," Lance said, "because they're quiet. They were up all night partying, man. Even after they dumped you down here, they were loud and wild for hours."

"How long have they been quiet?" Rick said.

"An hour or two. I haven't heard anything from up there. Not a peep, man. Nothing."

Rick wondered where Halperin and Joanne were and if they were okay. He was worried about Prai and Biak. He couldn't stand the thought of anything happening to Biak. He needed to get that man home safely to his wife.

He had to find a way to get all of them out of here.

Rick said, "We can try climbing, but after the bark, it's all mud. I don't know how safe that will be. Could cave in on us. Could bring the walls down. Being buried alive sounds like a horrible way to go."

"Agreed."

"We take it slow?"

Rick nodded. "Slow and easy."

"Are you hurt?"

"I can do this. You?"

"Ribs. Got to have a couple broken ones. Hurts to breathe. I'm okay, though. I'll be alright."

"You sure?"

"We stay down here, what is the alternative? They're going to kill us. Might torture us first. I'm not good with pain. That kind of pain. I can suck it up to climb out of here. That much I can do."

Rick was worried about being killed. He never thought about being tortured. He feared being cooked and eaten. Rick didn't think Lance witnessed the cannibalism. If he had, it would have been at the top of his list. "Okay. I say we sit, backs together, try climbing out with our feet."

Lance bit into his lip and grunted as he sat on the mud. "You think this will work?"

"Saw it in a movie," Rick said.

Lance was silent.

Rick laughed. "We are too far down to have me hoist you out."

They sat back to back. Rick pressed his feet against the bark wall.

"We've got a problem," Lance said.

"What's that?"

"I don't reach. My feet. My legs are too short. Are you touching? I can't--" he wiggled, groaned. "No, this won't work."

Rick wanted to feel disappointed. "I don't think it was all that good of an idea in the first place."

Lance turned around, slowly, with one hand on his side. His face showed his pain. His lips curled, his expression contorted into a grimace. "Nah, man. It was an idea. Right now, that's what counts."

"I've got another one."

Lance smiled.

Rick was loving the sunlight. Being able to see without rain ruined his vision. "Forget me cupping my hands and hoisting you up an extra three, maybe four feet. I'm gonna plant my hands on the wall, and you are going to climb right up my back. Stand on my shoulders. It's still not going to be high enough, but the walls are mud. You can dig in with your hands and feet easily. Everything's wet."

Lance stood up. His fists were poised on his hips. He spun around in circles, staring up at the hatch over the hole. "How hard do you think it will be to open that door-thing up there?"

"I have no clue." It wasn't worth worrying about. Climbing up to it was the first issue. "I had a knife."

"They take it?"

"Must have."

"The bars look like they're just tied with like weeds or something."

Rick squinted, staring up at the top of the hole. "They make houses in the treetops, Lance. My guess, they know how to tie a knot that won't come undone easily."

"We've got nothing to lose, do we?"

"Just time."

"Get against the wall, then. Spread 'em," Lance said. He tried to laugh. A sound did escape his lips. There was nothing humorous about it. Sounded more like a gasp.

Rick pressed his palms against the bark. He tried to get a good, steady stance.

"I'm going to, what, just climb up your back like a ladder? Isn't that going to hurt?"

"I imagine it might," Rick said.

"You ready?"

Rick nodded his head. "Let's do this."

Lance seemed apprehensive about how to start. He set his foot on the back of Rick's calf muscle, his hands on Rick's shoulders. "I don't know about this. What if I break your leg, or something?"

"Lance!" Rick ground his teeth. He didn't mean to shout. The last thing he wanted to do was draw attention to the hole. Shouting could do just that, draw attention. "Please. Climb. You're not going to hurt me."

There was what might have been considered a pause. Rick waited. He was just about to turn around when he felt Lance bounce on his calves. He felt himself sink into the mud some. The pain didn't come until Lance's knees were on his back. The bone rubbed against his spine.

"You okay?" Lance said.

Rick couldn't talk. He realized he was holding his breath. Lance might weigh more than he did. Slightly overwhelmed, he concentrated on keeping his balance. His hands were stuck against the wall. His body was angled in a way he wasn't sure he'd be able to move, or stand up straight.

Some of the weight lifted. Lance's knees were off Rick's back. His feet were getting nestled onto Rick's shoulders. "Okay, man. Okay. Now stand up. I have, like another, I don't know, seven or eight feet to climb. I can do this."

Rick stepped forward with his right foot. It was more like dragging his toe through mud. Once it was planted, he did the same with his left leg. He felt like Frankenstein learning to walk. A few more shuffles forward and he was up as straight and as tall as possible. "I can't lift you any higher than you are."

He took his hands off the wall and wrapped them around Lance's ankles.

"I'm good. I'm okay," Lance said. He had his hands buried into the side of the wall. He pulled himself up, all of his weight lifted off of Rick. He kicked a foot into the mud for a foothold. He dug at it with his toes. The mud slid where his hands had the wall. "Ah, geez. Oh, no."

Rick took a step back as Lance fell and landed flat on his back.

CHAPTER 26

Danny sat on what he'd call the porch of the team's hut. He was quiet as he watched Biak's wife watching him. He was no doctor, but he knew she was very pregnant. If he didn't know any better, he'd swear if she didn't deliver the child soon, she'd explode.

He saw what she held onto. It was a crutch, crudely constructed, but clearly a crutch. He figured the instrument was meant for him, but that she was too apprehensive about approaching the strange white man. He offered up a smile. He hoped that might help, because he wanted the crutch. His immobility was restricting.

He had no idea what her name might be but nodded and smiled a little brighter as she hesitantly took slow, small steps toward him. He waved a hello that he hoped came off as friendly and not creepy. He knew his smile had to look half-cocked, as the juice he'd been guzzling left him feeling more than just a slightly intoxicated. If nothing else came out of this adventure, he hoped to discover the tasty drink's recipe. He'd kill at parties. Kill.

As she got closer to the porch, he wanted to stand up. Greet the pregnant woman properly. He knew if he put any weight on his leg he'd crumble to the mud. The last thing he wanted to do was fall down and risk worsening his injury. He decided to simply continue waving and smiling.

She said something to him and pointed at his leg. She stuck the crutch under an arm and did a mock-walk with her weight on the crutch. Then she offered the crutch over to him.

"Thank you," Danny said. He spoke slowly and loudly, like that might help her understand English. Obviously it would not, but she did smile and nod. *Thank you* might be one of those universal phrases that even if you couldn't understand a foreign language, given the circumstances, it was clear.

The woman turned around.

Danny used the crutch, stood letting the strong wood support his weight. He tapped Biak's wife on the shoulder. "Um, my friends, they have been gone a while. All night. I'm kind of worried about them."

The slow, loud speech just afforded him more smiles and nods. She had no clue what he said.

He pointed to the hut behind him. "My friends," he said. He moved his hand around in a circle. "Friends. They are not back yet." The different hand gestures did little to add definition to his words. It became immediately frustrating, like playing charades with drunk people. He pretended to fish with an imaginary pole. "Friends," he said for a third time, to no avail.

Danny hobbled the few steps back and sat once again on the porch. Biak's wife nodded, turned, and walked away.

Rick and the others were okay. He'd promised Danny they were just going to fish this one last time and then everyone was going home. As good a fisherman as Rick was on the Great Lakes, it seemed his skill did not transfer across the ocean. The creature in the Wairoku was obviously not ready to be caught. He couldn't blame Rick for spending some extra hours on the water trying. His job may depend on it. Hell, Danny thought, with Lance out there competing to capture the creature first, all of their jobs might depend on it.

They were okay.

They'd be back soon enough.

Danny picked up the handcrafted pottery carafe of Poison Frog. He lifted it to his lips and as he took a long swallow, his eyes looked up to the sky. He did not get discouraged. The morning had been beautiful; the nicest day since they landed on this massive island. The grey clouds moving in weren't going to bother him. This was it.

They would be on their way home before long.

***

Tika fought every urge to run. She fought every natural instinct to scream for help. She moved from tree to tree the remainder of the night. Stopping at each tree, she waited several minutes, or until she was sure nothing was following, tracking her moves. She would take a deep breath and then slink her way to the next tree.

Many times she wanted to move further. Go faster.

One tree at a time. A few yards at once.

If any of the Yakti were in the area, they'd hear her. She needed to keep calm, cool, collected.

One tree at a time.

Eventually, just before dawn, she'd made it to the river. Her imagination did not settle down, not once. She knew why Rick and Lance were here. They were trying to catch a long-toothed and vicious fish. She knew if she tried to cross the river, it would get her. She knew she'd get attacked. No boats were along the bank. The water was swift moving. Little rapids. She knew that it was deep in spots, as well. Swimming across was not wise, but she couldn't think of another way--at least not without attracting unwanted attention.

If the fish didn't eat her, devour her flesh, then she'd drown.

The sun in the sky was false consolation.

Tika knew it was now or never. Rick and the others, if they were not dead already, did not have long left to live. She needed to hang onto the idea, at least, that they were still alive.

She stepped over a fallen tree. She stepped over broken branches and leafs, and took several steps closer to the water.

And stopped.

She had an idea. It was a little crazy, but it could work. She went back to the mound of brush. She climbed between the brush, squatted, and grabbed hold of as much of it as possible, and stood. She walked toward the bank with it. It would float and provide camouflage as she was carried down the river.

Tika walked right into the water. If she stopped to feel it or hesitated at all, she'd change her mind. Washing the pots, pans, clothing, and herself, she did not mind the water. She was never one for swimming. At the university, she swam in a crystal clear and amazingly well maintained pool. As soon as her feet hit the water, dirt kicked up and became murky, nearly impossible to see even her own toes.

She was knee deep and about to duck down and hide behind the branches she carried, clung onto, when she heard them.

Behind her.

The Yakti.

CHAPTER 27

Lance knelt in the far corner of the hole. He kept one arm tightly wrapped around his stomach while the other dug. He scooped out piles of wet earth and tossed it toward the other wall. He reminded Rick of a kid at the beach, one who had no pail or shovel, one without any brothers or sisters, and who played alone in the sand.

Rick sat with his back against the bark, knees drawn up, and just watched for several moments. Lance needed medical care. With broken ribs, the fall didn't help. It was a failed escape attempt, but at least for those moments they'd been trying. Things became bleak fast. The sun in the sky had been covered by a blanket of clouds. There was no way to gauge time. Only thing Rick knew for sure was that he was hungry and had missed several meals.

"What are you doing," Rick said.

Lance tipped his head from side to side, as if searching for the right words to use to answer Rick's question. "I have to piss."

Rick closed his eyes and sighed. "I am not seeing the connection."

"I have no idea how long we're going to be down here. Do you? No. Neither of us does. Could be hours, days, or weeks. We have no clue, right? Well, right now, I have to piss. You want me to just go anywhere? What about when we have to defecate?" Lance shrugged. "It's unpleasant to think about, but we need some kind of makeshift latrine. I figure if we go, then we toss a little dirt on top. An excrement layer cake, if you will."

"It's good thinking," Rick said. He could not imagine squatting over some dug hole.

"We really should make more of a trench along this wall. Better to think long term; like they plan to keep us down here a while. It also gives us something to do. Gets our minds off the situation," Lance said. He never turned around. He never stopped digging.

Rick sat for a moment longer before walking on all fours to Lance. He used the tips of his fingers to delve into the moist earth. Digging out a trench would be simple, mindless work. It would certainly give his mind a needed break from worrying about Joanne, Halperin, and the men he had come to think of as more than just guides.

Expending energy curbed Rick's appetite some. At first, anyway. Seemed the harder he worked digging out the latrine, the less hungry he felt. Again, that was at first.

"I'm sorry about how all of this turned out, you know."

Rick nodded. "You couldn't have known. I don't think even the Wairoku knew. No way that the guides would have taken us out if they even suspected this other tribe was going to attack."

There was no getting the thoughts of Curtis out of his mind. The sight of him on a spit, the smell of charred flesh. The memory, or nightmare, of the Yakti trying to force-feed him pieces of his friend's flesh.

"Nah, man. You know what I mean, with Karen and all."

"Rick stopped digging, arms elbow deep in mud. "I'm sorry, what   did   you   say?"

"The meeting was purely accidental. We talked at the bar--"

"Meeting?"

"At the awards dinner."

"This year? I --I'm not sure what you're talking about. Lance, what are you telling me?" Rick sat up straight, ass on his heels, hands on his thighs. "What the fuck are you talking about?"

Lance moved slowly. His lips were pursed. "She said she told you before you left. The two of you talked. That you knew."

Rick remembered the night the network told him about the planned adventure and getting home to tell Karen, a bouquet of flowers. . .and he remembered the car in his driveway. Something he should have confronted then, at that moment.

He hadn't.

He could tell people he just wasn't confrontational, but that was only partly true. He was a coward. It wasn't that he was afraid to fight, it was that he was afraid to lose. Lose the fight, lose his wife; lose his family, and lose all he'd worked for.

Rick just shook his head.

"I thought you knew. Makes sense now, why you've been nice, and helpful and civi--"

Rick threw a punch. It connected with the side of Lance's head near the temple. It couldn't have hurt much. The mud caked on his fist made the knuckles slide right off skin. It did catch Lance off guard, cut him off in mid-sentence.

There was no point in waiting. Lance would fight back. Rick threw himself forward. He wrapped his arms around Lance and drove him down onto his back.

Lance grunted. The broken ribs. Rick punched him in the chest. Once. Twice. He did not expect Lance to scream. The man yelled loud. The pain must have been excruciating. He hoped so. He didn't let up, except now he pummeled Lance in the face.

The shouting became like an echo. It boomed and filled his ears.

His fist broke the skin over Lance's eye, along a cheek, and had split and it fattened the man's lip. He was straddled on Lance's chest. It could not be easy to breathe, not at all.

Lance was not the one screaming.

Rick stopped. Thought it might have been him screaming.

It hadn't been.

The ruckus floated down from above, from the top of the hole.

The natives half hung over the waffle gate, arms waving, cheering on the brawl.

Brawl.

It wasn't. It was one-sided. Rick looked down at Lance. His eyes were open.

"I'm sorry," Lance said. He turned his head to the side, spit blood. It drooled off the corner of his mouth. "I am. I'm sorry."

Rick didn't want to talk. He wasn't about to forgive this man. He no longer felt like punching him, not anymore, not knowing that the Yakti received satisfaction watching. They were the Yakti's prisoners, not their entertainment.

"We're not here to amuse you," Rick said. He stared up at them, his fist in the air. "We're not here for your twisted entertainment."

"I'm sorry about everything, Rick."

"Shut the fuck up, Lance. We need to get out of here. When we escape this death, I'm going to kill you!"

The waffle gate over the top of the hole lifted. A knotted rope was dropped into the hole. The cackling from up top had stopped. Only one native, Painted Face, continued to talk.

Rick had no clue what was being said. What he did understand was the hand motion. Painted Face waved them up.

"They want us to climb up."

"They letting us go?" Lance said.

You better hope not, Rick thought. "You climb first. I'll follow you up."

Rick stood up. There was nowhere to wipe the mud off his hands. He was coated in it. The idea of being freed almost made him smile. The ladder initially looked *that* promising. Somehow, he couldn't accept that freedom was what awaited at the top of the rope. Instead, he dreaded the idea of climbing up and out of the hole.

CHAPTER 28

Blue skies were gone. Grey ones moved in. There was a chill in the air. It cut through the humidity. It was not raining. The forest had never felt more remote, nor had it ever looked as prehistoric. Rick did not expect to get off the island. He did not think he would make it home. He hoped, but was not counting on ever seeing his son Jared again.

The fire pit was empty, the spit moved. Prai, Biak, and Halperin were still bound to the trees. Rick wanted to close his eyes. He wanted to believe he was asleep. None of the men wore shirts. Their flesh was bruised, and faces swollen and bloody. Biak was the only one with his head still up, eyes open.

Prai and Halperin, their heads hung chins to chests. Rick wanted to call out to them, see if they were okay, but if he did, what would he say? What ray of hope would his yelling offer? Nothing.

Where was Joanne? Where were they keeping her?

"Rick!"

It was Tika. She was across from him. The Yakti had her on her knees. She was naked. Her body was battered and bruised. One eye was purple and swollen shut. Her hands were behind her back. Even from where he was, he could see that her wrists were bound. Anger filled him and it was released with tears. His lip quivered. "Are you alright?"

The natives spoke loud and fast. It looked like they talked to Tika. She nodded at them, and then looked back toward Rick.

"What did they say? What's going on?"

"They want you to fight," she said.

Painted Face walked into the center of the trees. The other tribesmen encircled their leader.

Rick looked at Tika. As he was led around the circle, he saw that her hands were bound to her ankles. She had been hogtied. His face felt flush. He bet his skin was red. He knew they'd be able to see his anger.

"They want me to fight *Painted Face?* I'll fight him. I'll take him on." Rick could not remember his last fight. It was in grade school. Timmy Slater threw his brown bag lunch on the playground floor and stepped on it. He did it every day for a week. That Friday, Rick stood up for himself. First, he refused to unhand his lunch. When Timmy snatched it regardless and crushed it under his heel, Rick punched the bully in the gut. His punch was lame. He'd held back, afraid of actually hurting another person. It got him a fat lip. Timmy did not hold back. He clocked him good, knocked him down with the blow. It happened in front of everyone, including Debbie Collins. The punch wasn't as bad as having her see him on his butt crying.

"Rick, it's not against him," Tika said.

A Yakti prodded his back, forcing him forward into the makeshift ring. Rick spun slowly around. There had to be forty or fifty people surrounding them. "Who, who do they want me to fight?"

Lance was pushed forward. He stumbled. He kept an arm around his ribs. "They must want us to fight."

Moments ago, that would not have been an issue. He would have gladly beat the piss out this man, but not now.

Rick shook his head. "I'm not fighting him."

Painted Face spoke. Rick hated the high-pitched whine of his voice. It ate through him.

Rick waited. He knew Tika would translate.

Painted Face went on and on. He talked with his hands, pointing and waving them around. He kept indicating Rick and Lance and pointing toward the river. He had no idea how Tika was going to repeat everything back to him.

"What's going on, Tika? What's he saying?"

"He says that the creature in the river has killed many of his men and women and children. The creature is a sign from the spirits, sent here to defend the tribe against pale skinned people, only it has become confused and is feasting on the wrong people."

Rick saw a chance. That slight glimmer of hope. "Tell them, Tika. Tell *him* why we're here. We are going to fish for it, and catch it. We are going to get it out of his river, and leave. We're here to help," Rick said.

"Rick," Lance said.

Rick held up his hand. "Shut up, Lance. We can get out of this. Act like a man. Act like we belong here, and that we're not scared to death. Puff out your chest."

"My ribs."

"Fuck your ribs. Coddle them later," Rick said. He kept his voice calm. He wanted to give the illusion of being in control of the situation.

"We're not getting out of this."

"They cooked Curtis, Lance. They fucking ate him last night. We're going to get out of this. We're going to get away from these people and go home." He heard himself speak. His tone of voice came across as confident and cocksure.

Tika began talking in her native tongue. Rick knew she was pleading, trying to sell the story.

Painted Face actually listened. He nodded at certain points of Tika's rendition.

When Tika finished, Painted Face erupted. He looked angry. His arms flailed and he ran around the inner circle, inciting the Yakti.

Rick stared at Tika. He waited for her to make eye contact. Whatever was being said, he knew it could not be good.

"I told him that where you are from you work with spirits, and that is why your skin is so white. The color was drained from fighting against demons. He calls you *Laleo*. You are ghost demons. He does not understand that there is a world beyond these trees. He has no concept of other countries."

"And?"

"And he does want your help. He wants to get rid of the creature in the water, same as Chief Amu. He believes the things I have told him. So, yes, he does want you to get rid of the creature, but just one of you."

"One of us? What's that mean?" Lance said.

"He says it is all about strength. The creature in the river is elusive and strong. It stalks before it attacks. When it strikes, it kills. You two are still going to fight. Whoever is not dead at the end of your battle will fish for the creature. You will be given two moons to catch it. If not, your limbs will be cut off and thrown in the river with the rest of your body as a sacrifice," Tika said. She never blinked once while delivering the message.

Lance bent forward and threw up.

CHAPTER 29

Danny Hughes heard the hoots and hollers. Something was going on. He watched the Wairoku run past his hut. They were headed toward the river. He almost laughed. It was about time. Rick had been gone far too long, and he was past beginning to worry. He had been all-out worried.

He used the crutch Biak's wife made for him and hobbled in the mud toward the gathered tribe. He had not wanted to hinder the success of the trip. The accident had been his fault, and the injury hurt his pride more than any physical pain he felt (although the Poison Frog deserved some anesthetic credit, he supposed). Point was that he was ready to go home. Enough was enough, and he had had enough.

The gathered Wairoku slightly parted, letting Danny through.

It wasn't Rick and the others waiting who had arrived.

It was Lance's guy, Tyson. Tyson McFadden.

An arrow protruded from his chest. Chief Amu stood next to him, and everyone stared at Danny.

"Tyson?"

"They were taken. All of them. I fell out of the pirogue when the arrow hit me. I thought I was dead. I woke up on the right side of the riverbank and made my way here. I tried to keep out of sight. There is so much shit in that jungle. I was out of my mind. I thought everything was going to eat me," Tyson said.

Danny pointed.

Tyson touched the arrow. "This? It hurts. Stings like a mother, but, I'm not bleeding. I thought these things were dipped in poison, right? I musta got hit with one that was lacking. Shit, I don't know. Maybe I'm dying and don't know it?"

"What about Rick?"

"Your guys? I have no clue. I didn't see them. I don't even know what happened to my friends."

A topless woman came over with a carafe. She offered it to Tyson.

"That's Poison Frog," Danny said. "Takes the edge off."

Tyson took a long swallow, wiped his forearm across his mouth. "What do we do now?"

"We have Chief Amu coordinate a rescue party."

Chief Amu's eyes went wider at the sound of his name.

"You speak the language? Because I don't understand a single thing they've said to me," Tyson said.

Danny spun around while he spoke. "I don't, but how hard can it be to get them to understand? They must know something's wrong. You've got an arrow sticking out of you, for heaven's sakes. No one is coming back from fishing, and they're living in a forest where every other tribe around is a natural enemy. They know something is wrong!"

* * *

Painted Face stood between Rick and Lance. He made some kind of declaration. Rick didn't bother to look at Tika. He could only imagine what had just been said: short, brief and to the point. It was more than likely something like, "And now, they will battle. . .to the death!"

Painted Face stepped out of the circle. He left Rick and Lance inside it. The chanting of the crowd began immediately. The drone of their voices matched one another. It felt almost hypnotic.

Rick assumed weapons would be thrown into their ring, but none were. Painted Face pointed at Rick and yelled.

"You have to fight," Tika said.

"What if we don't?" Rick said. He stared at Painted Face. He kept his air of confidence as best he could. It was the only lifeline he saw, so he held onto it with a death grip.

"He never said," Tika said.

It didn't require much imagination. If they didn't fight, they were both likely to be de-limbed and tossed into the river as a sacrifice. "Get your fists up," Rick said. He curled his fingers in and knuckles out. "Follow my lead."

Lance made fists. The two circled each other.

"What's your plan?"

"Hit me," Rick said.

"What? I'm not going to hit you."

"If you don't, Painted Face over there is going to have both of us killed, along with my friends. We need to make it look like we're fighting. Keep them happy while I try to think of a way out of this."

"A way out of this?" Lance threw a jab and hit Rick in the shoulder. Wasn't much behind the punch. He'd been hit harder playing punching games with the other boys in elementary school. "You think the cops are going to show up, huh? Troopers? The marines? We're fucked, Rick. This is it."

Rick tossed a lob of a punch toward Lance's face.

Lance sidestepped out of the way. "This is a fight to the death, Rick. They expect us to fight until one of us is dead. You know what that means? This isn't over until you or I stop breathing."

"I know exac--"

Lance threw a punch that connected solid with Rick's cheek. Skin split. Rick stumbled back several steps. He wiped blood using the back of his hand. "What the hell are you doing?"

"It's nothing personal," Lance said.

"What's not per--"

Lance charged forward, head down, arms out. He wrapped Rick like a football player and drove him onto the ground. Mud broke the fall.

Rick didn't want this. He knew they had to fight. He wasn't about to kill anyone.

Or, he hadn't been willing to kill anyone.

Lance changed the game. He struggled to mount Rick to stick his knees onto Rick's arms and pin them in place. Rick bucked, bowing his back. It didn't throw Lance off, but it did free up an arm.

Rick punched Lance in the side. He was shooting for the injured ribs. The punch landed, but it was the wrong side. Lance grunted, regardless. He leaned to the side, perhaps over exaggerating caution. Rick took advantage of it. He twisted underneath Lance's weight, and squirmed. He made it over onto his stomach and tried to crawl out from under Lance.

Rick felt a hand grab hold of his hair. His head was raised and slammed back down. It might be muddy. It didn't matter. It hurt. Rick couldn't scream or gasp. Lance wasn't letting him up. He was holding his face down.

He couldn't breathe.

Rick's lungs started to burn. If anything, he had assumed, he would have to take it easy on Lance. Carry him along. The man had broken ribs. He'd been proved wrong. Lance displayed his desire to survive.

Drawing up his knees, Rick pushed with feet. He was able to throw Lance off. Lance fell forward, his legs wrapping tightly around Rick.

Turning his head, Rick sucked in air. Mud dripped into his open mouth. It didn't matter. The air tasted twice as good as the grit on his tongue and teeth. He wanted to tell Lance to stop, not to do this.

Part of him knew he couldn't.

There was no stopping.

This needed to be done.

He was not going to kill Lance. He would, however, defend himself.

He worried, if Lance got the upper hand, he would kill him.

The man had already stolen his wife.

Karen.

He'd ruined his family.

Divided it.

Rick pulled at Lance's legs, twisting his body left and right. He needed to get free.

He wasn't going to think about Karen.

Jared.

He wanted to get out of this, and to make it home. His home. Nothing was set in stone.

He dug fingernails into Lance's legs, pulled the calf in close and bit down hard. He knew his teeth broke skin. He tore at the flesh as Lance screamed.

He wasn't the only one screaming.

The Yakti around him screamed and howled.

He'd excited them, roused their animal instinct. At first he thought he'd made a mistake in doing so. Now, he wasn't so sure. They seemed to love the fact that he'd eaten human meat.

He hadn't.

Rick didn't swallow anything. He spat out whatever was in his mouth.

The cheering, the howling, the chanting, it never stopped.

Rick pulled himself up Lance's legs, clawing his way toward his back. He dropped a punch onto the back of each thigh. Charlie horses. Lance kept twisting under Rick.

The ribs interfered with Lance's defense. Broken ribs weren't going to help his offense, either. Rick took advantage of every second afforded him.

Lance kept digging hands into the mud and pulling himself across the circle, an inch at a time. It didn't matter. Rick made progress, too. He was almost fully on top of Lance.

Then he saw it.

What Lance was crawling toward.

Axes.

There were two, not far ahead, but just out of Lance's reach.

The weapons hadn't been there when the fight started. Someone, most likely Painted Face, had tossed them in to add suspense and tension to the match. Increased viewer entertainment. These Yakti were no different from Americans. Fishing wasn't good enough. He had to head to Papua and fish for prehistoric creatures with huge teeth to make television watchers happy.

Rick drove a fist into the small of Lance's back. He moved up Lance's legs as if he was climbing a ladder and sent a short flurry of punches into his sides. Rick had no idea where the broken ribs were. Right now, it didn't seem to matter. Each blow delivered pain.

Lance, who had been reaching for the axe, stopped and brought his arm back and tucked it in as if hoping to deflect punches. He jabbed an elbow back, hitting Rick in the chest.

Rick grunted, stunned. Lance took advantage of the pause and spun over. The movement tossed Rick off of him. Lance got back on his belly and scurried forward. Tears streamed down his face as if every motion had sharp broken ribs sticking him in his lungs. He picked up the axe, just as Rick grabbed hold of his ankle.

Lance kicked out with his free leg. His foot scraped along Rick's knuckles. Rick let go and Lance jumped to his feet. He kept an arm draped across his midsection, the other held tightly to the axe's handle.

"You're going to kill me?" Rick said. He pushed himself up onto his knees. His knuckles bled. His face felt numb. He wasn't sure he had the strength to stand. He waved Lance toward him. "Come on, then. Let's do this." Lance kept re-gripping the handle of the axe.

He didn't charge. He seemed stuck in some perpetual contemplation. Every move critical.

Rick looked over at the second axe. It lay in the mud. Lance turned his head, as if to see what Rick saw. It was just a split second distraction. Rick jumped on it and lunged forward. This time he wrapped Lance up and drove him backward to the ground.

Rick screamed. The axe blade cut through the back of his thigh.

Without delay, Rick sat on Lance's chest. He positioned his knees on Lance's arms. They were pinned. It didn't seem to matter. Lance wasn't putting up much of a fight.

Rick's anger was expressed in his fists. He broke Lance's nose with the first punch. He dropped lefts and rights. Each punch did damage to Lance's face.

Lance was breathing but unconscious.

Painted Face hooted. He stepped into the ring and hollered.

He didn't need Tika to translate, not this time.

They wanted Rick to finish it.

Only one person could win.

Only one would walk away.

CHAPTER 30

"I'm not going to do it," Rick said.

Rick sat straddling Lance's chest. He slowly stood, hovering over the unconscious man. Blood bubbled in Lance's nostrils as he breathed in and out.

"You have to," Tika said. "If you don't, you are both dead."

Painted Face watched and listened to the exchange. He pounded a fist against his chest. He raised that fist into the air and shook it.

Rick closed his eyes. His leg throbbed. He did not want to show any weakness. He knew warm blood oozed from the wound. "This is over."

"Rick," Tika said.

Painted Face stomped toward Rick. He growled with each step. His brow furrowed. No eyes were visible, just the white stripes across his face. He pounded both fists against his chest and pointed down at Lance.

Lance moaned. He turned his head to the side. He was not currently a threat, Rick thought, but if his competitor woke up it could prove an entirely different story.

Rick looked at Painted Face. "We're not going to get out of this alive, are we? My killing Lance isn't going to save my life, hers, or theirs," Rick pointed at the trees that held Biak and Prai. "And where is Joanne? Where is my friend?"

Painted Face just listened, even cocked his head to the side. Perhaps the calm and soft tone that Rick spoke with caught him off guard, had him a bit off balance.

"You should just let us go. Have this be over with. I'll still fish, if you want. I'll still try to catch that monster in the river, but if there's one, there's more. I know that. You don't. You think it's a devil, a demon, but it's not. You and your people, you're just ignorant, that's all. Uneducated. It's not your fault. I'm not blaming you for being stupid, or hostile, or even cannibals. You don't know any better. You live in a jungle. You're like a demonic Tarzan on a steroids or something. I don't know. I wish I knew, but I feel helpless and clueless, and I know I'm rambling now. I just can't help but suspect I'm losing my mind here. That I--"

Painted Face snarled.

He lifted a leg and dropped the heel of his foot onto the side of Lance's head.

Painted Face pounded his own chest, again.

"Stop it!" Rick said, suddenly shouting.

Painted Face punched Rick in the solar plexus, and brought his foot down again on Lance's skull. Blood dripped from his ear.

"You're going to kill him!" Rick gasped, trying to breathe.

Painted Face had worked himself into a frenzy.

He jumped into the air and crashed down on Lance's head.

Rick pushed Painted Face.

The wiry man was all muscle. He did stumble backward but kept his balance. He ran at Rick, grabbed his head, and threw him to the ground. Rick let out a yell as Painted Face held him by his hair and dragged him closer to Lance's body.

Rick wanted to close his eyes. He knew what was coming. The crazy native was going to jump on his head until his skull caved and his brains were squashed. He didn't want his life to end this way. He did not want to die out here, away from his son.

He couldn't let that happen. There had to be a way to stop his own murder.

If there was some way to. . .

The axe.

It was right there by his head.

Rick reached for it. He raised it in the air and swung down, fast and hard.

The chanting around him stopped.

Everyone fell silent.

The only thing Rick heard was Tika. She was crying.

Rick knew he was safe. He got up onto his knees.

He'd survived. Painted Face would not kill him, not right now, anyway. He'd bought some time.

At what cost?

He put both hands on the axe handle and lifted it out of Lance's chest. The sucking sound made was not something he'd ever forget. He had no idea if Lance was dead. It didn't matter. He'd slammed an axe into another man.

He laughed.

Loud.

Hard.

He looked up at the bleak sky. He tasted the humidity. It filled his lungs. It would rain soon.

He cried.

The tears streamed.

He couldn't get it out. The cry caught in his throat. His mouth was wide open.

Rick bent forward. He stomach heaved. He vomited. So little was in his stomach. Slimy drool filled his mouth. It sagged off his bottom lip. He coughed and coughed again, trying to catch his breath.

Painted Face shouted.

Men came forward. They picked Rick up off the ground by the arms.

Rick had no words. If they planned to kill him, so be it. He deserved it. He wanted to die. He'd committed murder. Selfishly, he'd taken another life.

His hands trembled.

He could feel the sensation of the axe blade plunging into flesh.

He saw Painted Face through his tears. The warrior stood poised over Lance's corpse. He looked satisfied.

As Rick was dragged out of the circle, he noticed that Tika could not look at him. Her head was down.

"Where is Joanne," Rick said. He repeated it over and over. Each time, he spoke more loudly. "Tika, find out where Joanne is, please. We have to find out where they've taken her.

"Where is Joanne?"

***

Joanne was by the river. She reminded Rick of Tika. Joanne was naked and bruised. Purple marks covered her thighs and arms. Rick's mind went wild. He wanted to shut down his thoughts. He could not imagine her nightmare. She was hogtied, on her knees, with her head down. River water lapped at her skin.

Painted Face led them through the forest.

The sun was out. Rays shined down onto the swift moving water. It glimmered and sparkled.

The other natives followed behind Rick, and spread out along the bank. For the first time, Rick noticed children. Boys. Girls. They held hands with adults. How much had they seen?

Had they seen Rick kill Lance?

Did they look at him as if he were a murderer?

Even if they had witnessed the brutality, they would not consider him a killer. It was their way. How they were raised.

"Joanne!" Rick wanted to get her attention, and let her at least know she was not alone.

He limped more and more with each step he took. His leg ached. He knew nothing serious had been severed or he would have bled out already.

The heat was unreal. He was baking under the sun, even just for the few moments he'd been exposed.

Sweat mixed with mud coated his skin.

Rick turned his head left and right. He didn't see Tika.

"Joanne," he said, again.

She didn't look up, she didn't respond to the sound of his voice at all. He realized that she might be dead.

If she weren't kneeling, he'd swear she was.

"Joanne!"

Someone slapped the back of his head. It stung. His head was knocked sideways. He kept walking, didn't bother to turn around and look to see who had struck him. It didn't matter. He couldn't do a thing about it.

He did see his gear.

His poles and tackle box.

He saw Lance's, as well.

They wanted him to fish. What had they promised? He had two nights to catch the creature. Two.

The sun would set soon in an hour or so. Did this count as Day One?

There was not a way out. Even if he saw a chance to escape, he couldn't. There was no way he'd leave without Joanne, Tika, Biak, and Prai. He saw no way of both escaping and saving them first. He saw no way of saving himself.

The two days might end up feeling like an eternity, but that didn't matter. He was going to Hell anyway. Straight to Hell. There was no salvation, no forgiveness for what he'd done. There was no redemption.

Painted Face picked up Rick's fishing pole, and held it out. He spoke, grunting words through clenched teeth. What Painted Face said came out so archaic, there was no way he used actual words. He sounded nothing like Tika when she spoke.

Something sharp poked him in the back. He jumped forward. He reluctantly reached for the fishing pole. Painted Face did not let go. Instead, he pulled it toward himself, Rick along with it. Nose to nose, Painted Face did more grunting.

Rick was done caring. Over Painted Face's shoulder, he saw Joanne. She was not dead. Her eyes were open. They were locked on his.

His heart broke.

Rick tugged on the fishing pole, taking it from Painted Face's hands. This time Rick grunted first.

He was keeping the Yakti chief off balance with his behavior. He knew it.

Rick checked his box for bait, but there was none.

Painted Face yelled.

Rick turned around.

Lance was in the mud. They'd brought his body along. Rick clapped a hand to his stomach as a Yakti knelt by the body and used a knife to cut away chunks of meaty flesh. The cuts were placed in the palms of another's hands and were then walked over to Rick.

His new bait.

Painted Face spoke, looking at Tika.

Rick waited.

Tika said, "The creature feeds on human flesh. You must use human flesh to catch it."

She talked without looking up.

Rick looked over at Joanne.

The man thrust the pieces of Lance toward Rick. The bile backed up in his throat. He wasn't going to allow himself to get sick. He pierced the meat with his hook, and walked knee deep into the water. The current was powerful. He got his footing and cast his line.

Everyone was behind him, watching.

They were silent.

He tried to imagine that he was alone. Home. Maybe it was the Genesee he stood in. Maybe this was just a dream.

Hours might have passed, or minutes.

There were tiny tugs on the line. A monster wouldn't nibble. It would chomp. It wasn't the creature he sought. Still he waited, and when he was confident it was time, he yanked back on the pole and cranked the reel.

The fish fought. The hook caught.

The battle was simple. Far too easy. Rick reeled in his catch. Rainbow. Couple of pounds. Hardly a monster. Worse, it had eaten the bait.

Rick freed the fish, tossed it back into the river.

Painted Face grunted, splashed into the water and pushed Rick. He went down. Dropped his pole. The current caught it. Rick jumped forward and went under. His hands missed the pole, and helplessly, he watched it quickly carried away.

They had his legs and yanked him back toward the bank. The tug forced his head underwater. The sounds around him rumbled as water filled his ears, his mouth. He swallowed some. As they pulled him out of the water, he coughed, spitting up some of what he'd yet to swallow.

Painted Face punched him. It felt like a rock smashing into the side of his head. Black and white orbs floated in his field of vision. They dragged him out of the water. His shirt tore. Painted Face ripped the rest of it off his back.

Yakti held Lance's fishing pole. Meat dangled from the hook.

Rick shook his head. "No. No. Absolutely not."

An arrow slammed into the Yakti's eyeball. Blood spewed from the wound. The native dropped Lance's pole. He collapsed onto the mud.

Rick threw his hands up over his head.

More arrows came at them.

Wairoku were on the opposite bank. Rick couldn't see them, but knew, just knew it was them.

Yakti fell around Rick.

Painted Face ran. He stopped next to Tika and pulled a knife.

Rick screamed.

The severed rope around Tika's ankles fell free. He hoisted her up by the bound wrists and disappeared into the woods.

Rick saw several dead Yakti around him. He saw dead children as well. He had no idea how many arrows had been loosed, but enough to damage the barbaric tribe.

Pirogues were set in the water. The cavalry was coming. Rick had never felt so relieved.

It wasn't over.

Not yet.

CHAPTER 31

Rick picked up the knife the Yakti used to cut meat from Lance's corpse and dashed into the thicket of the forest. He was not going to stop until he found Tika.

He heard each of his heavy footfalls as they crashed onto brush and branches. Snapping twigs and the rustle of disturbed leaves echoed around him.

His breathing was done in quick and shallow breaths. His lungs burned. The laceration along the back of his thigh throbbed. He knew he was still bleeding. A moment ago he'd felt weak, like he couldn't survive even another minute. He'd been so close to complete surrender that he could not understand how he could now feel so rejuvenated.

Adrenaline.

It surged through his system with every fast beat of his heart. He worried the muscle would explode.

He jumped a fallen tree limb. His hands shot out to hit trunks to keep from crashing into them. His body screamed to his mind.

It was suicide. Every step he took brought him closer to certain death. This was Yakti territory. They'd regroup and come at the Wairoku for sure, but before that attack they'd find him -- lost in the forest.

He didn't stop. He pumped his legs harder, running faster.

Then he saw them not that far ahead of him. Tika was slowing down Painted Face's escape. Whether on purpose or not, Rick was thankful.

Painted Face reached their village. Tika's hair was in her face. He had her by the arm.

"You're not going to get away!"

They stopped, and Painted Face looked back. He made a face, eyebrows wrinkled. Maybe he didn't realize he was running from just Rick, his one-time prisoner.

Rick stopped. He stayed still.

It was in his peripheral.

Painted Face threw Tika to the side. She fell hard. She looked dead.

Rick had to focus on his main adversary. That was what was in front of him.

Painted face had a knife.

Rick held his up, gripping it tight. He wanted the native to know he was also armed. It would be a fair fight. They could both cut the shit out of each other. He didn't care.

He didn't care because he saw Tika get up. She made her way to the poles where Halperin, Biak, and Prai were. She would free them. He knew she would.

And he would deal with Painted Face.

One way or another.

He tried not to look to his left. It was there. He knew it. He felt like it watched him. Waiting.

Painted Face let out a battle cry. He charged.

Rick wasn't sure how to avoid getting stabbed or slashed. The only thing he could think to do in defense was drop to the ground, which he did at the last possible second. Painted Face flew over him, tripping on Rick's legs.

The man somersaulted and was back on his feet before Rick could get up.

Painted Face jumped into the air.

Rick rolled, got to his knees, and forced himself to stand. He leaned forward, holding the knife low in his right hand. "Come on, bad boy. You want some of this? You want a piece of me?"

He saw something in Painted Face's eyes.

Terror.

The native was not afraid of Rick.

Rick had nearly forgotten. It was behind him. It was running. He heard it as he launched himself as far to the right as possible.

The Cassowary had its head lowered as it charged. It ran right past Rick. It's bone-helmet head slammed into Painted Face's back.

The bird stood up straight.

Painted Face had been thrown several feet from the impact. The native slowly got to his feet. He held his hands up and backed away. He spoke to the bird. It was the first time Rick did not hear any grunt, anger or seething in the tone.

The Cassowary looked at Rick before he ran at Painted Face. The bird stopped a foot from the native.

If Rick blinked, he would have missed it.

A clawed foot kicked Painted Face. It was more of a slashing. Painted Face's midsection split open. His bowels spilled from the gaping hole.

Painted Face planted his hands over the hole, trying to pull the skin closed, attempting futilely to keep his life inside his body.

The Cassowary spun around. Rick had no clue how fast these birds ran. He'd try to get away.

He didn't have to.

The bird turned to his right and trotted off into the forest.

Rick stood statue still for several seconds. He could no longer see the bird, nor could he hear it. He could not believe what he'd just seen.

"Rick! Rick! Follow us!"

Tika had the others. The three men leaned on each other for support. "Let's go. Now!"

***

The pirogues were where they'd left them. Rick pushed one into the river and held onto it while Tika helped the others climb aboard.

Joanne.

"I have to go back," Rick said.

Tika grabbed his arm. "You can't."

"Joanne is still back there. They have her."

"Trust that my people have saved her. That was why they came. The Wairoku are not violent. They are here to rescue all of us," she said.

Rick almost couldn't look her in the eyes. The pain was as visible as the mud that dirtied her skin.

He looked toward where they had come from and hoped against all hope that Joanne was safe.

He climbed onto the pirogue and pushed off with a foot. "Is everyone okay?"

No one spoke.

Rick touched his boss on the shoulder. Halperin looked up. His eyes were black and blue, nose swollen.

Stopping between Biak and Prai, Rick tried to smile.

Both men smiled at him as if their cuts and bruises didn't matter, and they were back on the clock.

The river took them. They drifted out to the center of the river. Tika started the outboard motor.

CHAPTER 32

The Wairoku village looked more remote and isolated than ever. It was eerie. The animals of the forest were even silent. Rick strained to hear something, anything, as a sign of life.

They cut the motor and coasted up to the dock. Rick jumped onto the small pier and tied off the pirogue.

The others stayed on the boat.

"I'll check the area." There was no telling how the fight behind them had wound up finishing. While the Wairoku held the element of surprise, it wouldn't take long for the Yakti to re-group.

However, they were without their Painted Face leader. Someone would step up and fill the void. Someone was always anxious for the chance to lead.

"We're safer going with you."

They climbed out of the pirogue and lined up behind Rick. He still had his knife. He held it out in front of him like a flashlight. Its prehistoric-like blade did little to pacify his fear.

"Rick!"

It was Danny.

He came out of the forest on a crutch. Rick dropped the knife.

He could not explain how he felt. It moved him. Tears welled up in his eyes. He ran forward and embraced his friend. He had been ready to die, had expected death. "You're alright," he said.

Danny held Rick by the shoulders. "Me? I'm fine. I've been worried about you guys. I thought you were all dead. Where's Joanne?"

Joanne.

Rick pursed his lips. "I don't know."

"We need to get these guys to a bed," Tika said.

Danny tried to help. They assisted everyone to Rick's hut.

At the doorway, they stopped.

Prai's wife stood on the porch. She held something cradled in her arms. Prai's eyes opened wide. Rick clapped a hand on his shoulder. The guide took a step forward. Another. He looked weak. His knees trembled. Rick ducked under his arm and supported the man's weight. Prai's wife came off the porch. She walked toward them, the tiny baby swaddled in cloth. She spoke to Prai and Rick.

Tika translated. "You brought my husband home. I am forever thankful. Grateful that you kept your word and have returned to me the man I love. I would like to honor you by naming our first born son, Rick."

Silence surrounded them. Her words sank in.

Prai hugged Rick. Tight. Rick felt tears wet his skin, streaking through the caked mud.

"He's saying, 'Thank you,'" Tika said.

Rick felt overwhelmed. He did not want the hug to end. It felt safe, secure. All around them had been fear and death. "Go and hold your baby," Rick said, finally pulling out of the embrace.

They entered the hut. On one of the beds Tyson sat shirtless, his shoulder and chest bandaged. "Oh shit, guys."

"Sit, sit," Rick said.

Tyson did not listen. They got Halperin and Biak onto beds.

There were far too many things that could and shouldn't be said out loud. So instead, everyone took advantage of the moment and said nothing at all. The sound of silence was priceless.

***

They heard a commotion. People were chanting and screaming.

Rick held up his hand. "No one move. I'll check it out."

He walked to the hut's door. Outside, he saw natives. He hated to admit it, but he could not tell for sure if the Wairoku had returned, or if the Yakti were out there about to attack.

"It's them," Tika said.

Rick's stomach lurched at the thought the Yakti had follwed them.

She stepped around Rick and ran out, embracing a group of people.

Rick's breath caught in his lungs.

He left the hut slowly, as if in a daze, and then he jumped down from the porch to the mud. "Joanne," he said.

She was still naked.

The Wairoku had nothing to cover her with. Rick ran to her and hugged her tight. "It's okay. We're going home. It's going to be alright now."

CHAPTER 33

The media filled the airport. Camera flashes and video journalists captured everything from the plane landing to those who exited.

The police were there as well. They'd been contacted by Indonesia's American Embassy. Although statements and depositions had been taken and video recorded, U.S. authorities wanted their own.

There were going to be interviews and funerals. Rick did not look forward to seeing Curtis' family. He'd met the young man's parents a few times at summer cookouts, and when they came down to watch the filming of an episode. They were always proud of their son. He knew they received the news of their son's death from the embassy. They were not here at the airport. Not after they had been informed no remains were being shipped home.

Rick walked into the terminal. He kept Joanne close, an arm around her. He tried to shield her from the photos being taken. Microphones were thrust at them from every direction.

He watched Tyson push past reporters and run into the arms of a young woman. They kissed and hugged. He held her face close and talked quietly, but passionately to the woman. Rick could only imagine the intensity of love conveyed.

"We'll be giving a statement to the media shortly. Please, for now, I'm asking that you respect our privacy. Give us a moment to connect with our loved ones. Please," Rick said. He'd talked to Harry Krantz on the phone from the embassy. They were going to meet in the morning. The thirty plus hour flight had proved more grueling than anticipated.

The wounds were deep and would take a lifetime to heal.

Karen stood just beyond the media. Jared was cradled in her arms. The sight of them hit Rick hard. She was crying, chewing a fingernail.

Rick's pleas to honor their request for privacy were ignored. So many photos were being taken that it was like being stuck in a dance club with strobe lights.

Rick stepped away from Joanne just long enough to hug his family.

Nothing was fixed.

Nothing the same.

Rick took Jared into his arms and squeezed him tight.

"We've been so worried," Karen said. She sobbed. "We thought we'd lost you. When I received the call from your boss, I didn't know what to think. I've never felt so confused and scared."

"You look like you've grown a foot since I've seen you," Rick said.

The depositions surprised him. He did not mention killing Lance Crowley. He did not tell authorities about plunging an axe deeply into the man's chest. He blamed the death on Painted Face, saying that the crazed native had murdered the fisherman. He knew if Halperin told a different story, there would be an inquisition. He'd held his breath waiting to be arrested.

He wasn't. It never happened. Eventually, he exhaled and slowly began breathing normally. In the back of his mind, he still expected cuffs to get slapped onto his wrists at any moment, right up until he exited the plane.

Turns out Halperin didn't know Rick fought Lance.

He'd been unconscious during the fight. Never saw a thing. The only ones who had witnessed the brutal and deadly battle were his Wairoku guides and Tika.

It was getting away with murder. Rick tried not look at it that way. He'd lied to the police in Indonesia, and he planned to lie to the police here. He was not going to prison for surviving in a jungle. His hand had been forced. Lance turned the tables and came at him hard. It had been self-defense, pure and simple. In time, he was confident he could convince authorities, but how long would that take? If authorities ended up not believing him, would a jury. He wasn't going to risk life in prison for defending his life. The deadly force applied was essential to his own survival. He knew that. He understood the truth, and over time, he would convince himself that he was right.

The old Rick might have confessed. The man he had become wouldn't allow it.

"Rick?"

"What?" Rick said. He kissed his son's checks, and the top of his head.

"Why aren't you talking to me?"

Rick held his son so one ear was against his chest, the palm of his hand covered the other. "I want a divorce."

CHAPTER 34

When Rick entered the office, he saw that Harry Krantz was dressed in a suit and looked more dapper than ever. Brent Halperin had been seated on the corner of Krantz's desk in jeans and a pullover shirt, no tie, and rose he when he saw Rick.

"Rick, how are you?" Halperin extended his hand.

Rick shook it. "Good. How's the leg?"

"It's healing." Halperin pulled him in for a hug. "Hope you're doing okay?"

"I am." Rick knew Halperin had changed. He was no longer the same man. Halperin clearly cared about Rick's well being.

"Anything you need, you call me and not about just work, okay? I mean anything."

"I appreciate that." Rick knew Halperin felt indebted to him. He wanted that to stop. Truth was, saving Tika and Joanne, had been his priorities. He'd never admit that to anyone. He did not even like hearing the thoughts roll around inside his brain. They made him uncomfortable. Truths like this often did. "But I'm good."

There was small talk. Rick wasn't sure Krantz appreciated the weight of everything that happened during the filming.

"Halperin was telling me how the guys had their penises pushed all the way into their bodies? I can't even imagine that!" Krantz shuddered.

"It was different," Rick said, hoping he sounded diplomatic, and masked his disinterest.

"Thing is," Krantz said, "I'm just thankful Danny had his cassettes with him and that Curtis and Joanne's equipment was still on those boats when you escaped those savages."

"Pirogues."

"Savages, pirogues. Whatever."

"No, sir. The boats. They're called pirogues." Rick's eyes met Halperin's. They shared a knowing look.

Krantz shrugged. "It's a good thing, though. We're all very lucky. I've seen a lot of the raw footage, and even some that's been edited with your voice overs, and the segments where you read from your journal. Those journals turned out to be a top notch idea, don't you think?"

Rick nodded. "Best idea."

"You will also be happy to know that the U.S. Fish and Wildlife will be working with the Papua Conservation teams to research and tag, and learn about the fish. Not much they're going to be able to do about it. At least they are aweare and can begin to understand what has infested their fresh waterways. Thanks to you, to your team. And while we're on that subject, what is this fish exactly? What are they dealing with?"

"It's called a Goliath Tigerfish. It's African. It has no business in Papua. Yet, there they were. The footage Curtis was able to capture showed the staggered teeth, *at least* three inches long. The fish we fought was a beast. Six feet long, one-hundred and seventy-five pounds, at least. Also, a slight anomaly even among their breed. It's an aggressive fish. Eats any fish it can overpower. At that size, most men won't stand a chance. The Goliath clearly will always have the upperhand. I explained it to Chief Amu before we left. This fish could die out. It may not like the environment. Or, it will thrive. I don't suspect it will always be a threat to people. It is just trying to figure things out. Only consolation I could offer him was to have everyone be safe when down by the water. It took a while to convince him that it was not a spirit in the river. That it was just a fish. I think he got it. I hope he gets it."

"I can't wait until this series airs, Rick. Catch and Release has a ton of new sponsors. The sensationalism created by the press has money coming at us from every direction. We're putting together commercial promos that we're going to start running on every network over the next several months. We're going to build so much anticipation . . ."

"And you are dedicating the show, the series, to Curtis."

Krantz nodded. "Wouldn't have it any other way."

"Have you talked to his parents?" Rick said.

"I have. They're holding a memorial service on Monday."

"They won't return my calls," Rick said.

"They mentioned that. They're just not ready to talk to you. Not yet."

"They blame me."

Halperin shook his head. "I was there. I tried to tell them what it was like. They won't talk to me anymore either."

"Just give them some space. Some time. They have a lot to come to terms with. I know you understand," Krantz said.

Rick turned away, and looked out the window. Wasn't much of a few, only a half-full parking lot, and an expressway beyond that. "I understand."

***

Rick had a few moments before it was time to pick up Jared for the weekend. He sat in the recliner by the small bookcase. The one-bedroom apartment he rented was small, but comfortable. The bedroom was Jared's. All of his clothing and a bed just for him were in there. Rick slept on the sofa in the living room, even on the nights when Jared was with his mother.

He reached for his journal. He opened it to the last entry. The one he made on the plane ride home from Papua.

Rick Stone Journal Entry:

Tika stood beside me at the airport. The last few days dealing with foreign red tape overwhelmed and wore out all of us. I did not want to say goodbye to this woman. I knew what waited for me at home. I knew what was about to happen to my marriage. There was no way around it. The love was gone. Resentment had set in. And. . .

I did not want to say goodbye to this woman.

She was strong and brave.

And I had fallen in love with her. She might not feel the same way. I couldn't blame her if she hated me. Everything that happened was my fault.

Everything.

I didn't cast blame on anyone.

It was mine. All mine.

I'd be remiss if I didn't ask. I knew she had a visa and could come to the U.S. with us. She had her own life to live, her own dreams to chase, but after everything, I still felt selfish. I wanted her home with me.

She didn't come right out and say no.

This surprised me.

She still had a hard time looking me in the eyes. I know she felt ashamed for what had happened to her. I told her numerous times that none of it was her fault. Not one thing.

She'd cried that first night after we left the forest and the Wairoku people behind. Her head stayed on my chest for an hour. I thought she'd fallen asleep standing up.

She hadn't.

So I asked her then, for the first time, to come back to the U.S. with me.

Karen stood in the doorway of Rick's house as he carried his son from it to the car.

Rick didn't turn back and wave, he strapped his son into the car seat and kissed the top of his head. He smiled up at Rick. It was that smile that kept him alive. Jared, and Jared alone, was the reason Rick claimed for not being dead.

He knew this.

Rick pulled out of the driveway. He could see Karen in the rearview mirror, still in the doorway, still waving.

He put the car into gear and drove away.

It was a fifteen minute ride from Greece to Brooks Avenue on I-390. Traffic was light for a Saturday afternoon. Rick maneuvered around other cars and parked where directed, along the curb behind the taxis.

His neurotic behavior made him notoriously early. However, it paid off.

Rick got out of his car and walked around to the front. Standing on the sidewalk, she smiled.

"How was your flight?"

"Long," Tika said. "It felt like forever."

Rick opened his arms. She went slowly into them, and wrapped hers around him. She was going to need time, and healing. He wanted to give both to her, while staying as close as possible.

"This is America?" She said.

"You're going to love it here."

"I am not going to lie. I am a little scared."

So am I, he thought. "It's going to be alright. I promise."

THE END

About the Author

Phillip Tomasso is an award-winning author of numerous novels and short stories. He works fulltime as a Fire/EMS Dispatcher for 911. As the father of three, he spends any spare time with his family, writing and playing guitar. He is hard at work on his next novel.

www.phillipytomasso.com
phillip@philliptomasso.com
@P_Tomasso (Twitter)

Special Thanks

No book writes itself. I have so many people to thank. I hope I do not leave anyone out. First, to my Beta Readers: Janice McFadden Mickolas, Bobby Vachio, and Christine Houser. Next, I would like to thank my proofreader, Linda Tooch. I would like to thank Gary, and Severed Press. The love and support of family, friends, and readers is humbling. Thank you.

<u>Novels</u>

Mind Play
Tenth House
Third Ring
Johnny Blade
Adverse Impact
The Molech Prophecy (as Thomas Phillips)
Convicted
Pigeon Drop
Vaccination
Evacuation
Preservation
Sounds of Silence
Treasure Island: A Zombie Novella
Damn the Dead (Forthcoming from Severed Press)